The Hidden Agent

Joseph J. Cox

Published by Big Picture Books

Modiin, Israel

Note: In this book, the word G-d is used. It is not spelled out of respect and to copies of it from being placed in the garbage or otherwise disrespected.

Cover Photography from Andre Hunter at UnSplash.com

www.JosephCox.com

Dedicated to my children, for whom I wrote it.

Thank you to my most active Beta-Readers: Yedida, Michael, Rebecca, Shai, Susan and Isaiah. Thank you for making my work stronger.

Arrest

Sunday – 11:48 AM

The subway screeches to a halt as it comes into the station. I glance out the window and see the words I'd been expecting: "Prospect Park."

I feel ridiculous, taking a subway to make an arrest.

The doors open and I walk out, trying to act as if I'm just one of the crowd. It isn't hard. As a medium-sized black woman, I fit in easily with those around me. I glance around quickly, spotting my team members. There are five of them, all large white men selected by the FBI for their unarmed combat abilities. They've been assembled to back me up on this operation.

I don't really know them, but I'm glad they have my back.

The crowd surges through the warm and damp air of the subway. As a mass, we push through the turnstiles and rise up the stairs at the station's exits. We emerge into an unusually warm and brightly lit spring day. That's when I see the first of the minders. He is a tall African man with dangerous looking eyes. He scans the faces of everybody coming up the stairs. His eyes connect briefly with mine.

I think I see a flicker of recognition.

I hope it is my imagination.

There's a massive traffic circle across the street from the station. The circle is so large, it has a little park in the middle, with trees and a couple paths crisscrossing through the center of it. Where those paths meet, I can just make out a little war memorial; a black granite block surrounded by the rush of cars.

The little traffic circle reminds me of the FBI's memorial. It is a ridiculous digital kiosk they call the "Wall of Honor." You can use it by scrolling through the images and stories of those who have died in the line of duty. It has been designed so that it complies with the Americans with Disabilities Act. It resembles a large ATM.

With an involuntary shudder, I turn away from the little memorial. I don't want to end up as a photo and story captured forever within the "Wall of Honor."

The park in the middle of the traffic circle is tiny. But Prospect Park isn't small, it's massive. That's where the crowd is heading. A few policemen have stationed themselves at the crosswalk, between the station and Prospect Park. They aren't there to arrest anybody, though. Instead, they step into the street. With whistles and hands, they bring the rush of cars to a stop. The people from the subway surge forward, cross the street, and enter Prospect Park itself.

As we walk into the park, the noises of the traffic fade. I can smell the grass. I can hear birds. The sunlight is dappled by the trees. I pick up bits of the excited conversation that surrounds me.

I hear one word, again and again: "blessing."

I feel a little wave of anger every time I hear it. Anger, and pity. Pity for those who have been blinded and anger at Aji Abakar, the man who has blinded them.

We walk for only a few minutes before we come to a high fence along the left side of the path. I knew the fence would be here. I've known for weeks. But, still, it makes me nervous. The fence is in the way. The FBI can bring some heavy backup to bear. An armed response team, complete with rifles and armored vehicles. The fence, and the crowds, will slow them down. The fence makes everything riskier.

I line up with the others and together we walk towards the metal detectors under the careful eyes of yet another African minder. There are no tickets. There is only security. As we shuffle forward, I'm careful *not* to take any particular notice of my team members. I know they're there, but I don't want a simple flick of my eyes to alert event security to their presence.

When my turn comes, I open my backpack for inspection. I'm not carrying a gun. None of my team have guns. In fact, we only have two things the security guards would care about. The first is our FBI badges. I need mine to make the arrest and my team need theirs as a form of insurance – most people will think twice before assaulting a federal officer in a public space. We're not worried about the security team finding our badges, though. They aren't checking wallets. We knew they wouldn't be. We've watched them do this before.

The second thing they might find interesting is the tiny radio transmitter that has been inserted subcutaneously in my upper arm. The broadcaster is there so if things go really badly, my location can be tracked. The transmitter is too small for a metal detector to pick up. If you started caring about things that size, you'd have to freak out about every metal button and zipper. The cool thing about the transmitter is that a radio scan won't pick it up either. When my heart rate is normal, it broadcasts a short burst only about once every 15 minutes. As my heart rate accelerates, though, the broadcast rate picks up. If things are fine, I'd have to be very unlucky for them to detect the transmission. But if I start getting worked up, then I can be tracked far more easily. The technology is brand new; the FBI is taking this case seriously.

As expected, security doesn't notice my badge or the transmitter. I pass through the gap in the fence without any problems. If the minders actually recognized me, there's no sign of it.

As I walk into the park, I allow myself another look around. Each of my team members have an assigned spot. I expect to see them walking towards theirs. But I don't see them. I figure they must be behind me.

I keep walking forward, towards a prime spot just in front of the stage. Then I take a little collapsible stool out of my backpack. I take a seat. I start watching the crowd around me just like anybody else would.

But I still don't see my team.

Did the minders spot them? I can't exactly ask. The only transmitter I have is in my arm and it doesn't take questions. So, not knowing what's happened, I turn and try to calmly face the stage.

A Latina woman sits down next to me. She has a baby with her, passed out cold. I glance towards her and she smiles back at me. "Bless you," she says, her smile suddenly seeming to occupy most of her face.

"Bless you," I say back, as convincingly as I can manage.

Where the heck is my team?

"You're here early," she says. I wonder for a moment if she's part of some sort of secondary vetting system. Sit in the front row and the innocent-looking Latina girl will interrogate you.

"I just *needed* to see the man in the flesh," I say. A half-truth is always more convincing than a complete fabrication. It also happens to be the right thing to say. I know this because we've recorded thousands of conversations among Aji's followers. We may not know how they operate, but we know how they talk.

"I get that," the young woman says. She nods, thinks for a moment, and then asks the question I know is coming, "So, how has he touched *your* life?"

"He's why I'm in New York," I say with a smile.

"Oh?"

"Yeah," I say. "I was kind stuck in my career. I wasn't going anywhere. I didn't really know what to do with my life. I started watching Aji and I actually gave a little donation to his organization – I couldn't think of what else to do. You know? Next thing I know, I caught a big break. I got hired by a major organization here in New York."

"What do you do?"

"I'm a curator," I say. I do actually have a degree in Art History.

"Really?" she asks, "Where?"

"The Met," I say.

"Cool," she says.

"Yeah, you may not believe this, but I used to curate the Penguin Museum in LA." I laugh a little, "We had 30,000 penguin-themed and penguin-related items. People loved it, but I wasn't really giving them anything worthwhile. Now... well now I see those kids in the museum and I feel like I'm connecting them to thousands of years of culture and history and – well – it *has* to open their eyes and broaden their worlds, right?"

The young woman nods. "Yeah, I think so."

She pauses again for a moment. As if considering her next question. She tips her head towards the baby in her arms. "How old do you think he'd have to be to get something out of a visit?"

"Oh, any age will do," I say, "You never know what little minds learn when they're exposed to art and culture."

She purses her lips and nods in agreement. "Maybe I'll see you later this week."

"Oh, you probably won't see *me*," I say, "I mostly work in the back; with the collections that aren't on display. I'm hoping to work on the active exhibitions, I'm just not there yet."

"Oh, okay," she says. She's a little disappointed.

We sit there for a moment. I sneak another glance around, hoping to see at least one of my team members. But nobody is there. It has been five minutes. Somehow, they've been detained for five minutes. Do I abort? Can I abort? If the event security knows who I am, I may not make it out of the park.

I turn back towards the young Latina woman.

"How did he touch you?" I ask.

She smiles down at the bundle in her hands.

I get her meaning.

"A baby? How'd he manage that?" I ask, trying to suppress the subversive tone in my voice. The dirty joke just wants to leap out.

She doesn't notice my tone. I knew she wouldn't. She's all in.

She's smiling now, a bittersweet smile. I see tears come to her eyes.

"My husband was a cop," she says.

"Was?"

"Yeah.... He was killed in the line of duty. Some kid walked up next to his car and just shot him."

"That's horrible," I say. And I mean it. I am, after all, a cop.

"Yeah... I had all my family around afterwards. But I still felt all alone. My mom watches Aji. I didn't know what else to do. So, I did too. I saw his show. I wanted my husband back so bad. I said that if I could have my husband back, I'd share *that* story with everybody I knew. I'd praise the Lord and I'd share Aji's message with *everyone*."

5

"And?"

"Well, it turned out I was pregnant. I learned it two weeks after my husband died. This boy is my husband's boy."

She pauses, drawing in a deep, shuddering, breath.

"We'd been trying to have a kid for years."

I can't help but smile with her. I reach over and give her a little hug, trying not to squish the baby.

As we pull apart, she giggles. "It's crazy, isn't it. Here I am hugging a total stranger – a curator at the Met no less – in a park. And it's all because of Aji."

"It's crazy," I agree. *That* isn't a half-truth. As far as I'm concerned, it's crazy that coincidence breeds blindness.

I glance around again, but my team still isn't there. I know now that they aren't coming. They must have been blocked by security. This leaves me with a question: do I get up and walk away? The park is filling up. I've got five hours more before the main event and then there's Aji's show. Six hours of danger, without backup, to make a single arrest.

The other options run through my mind.

Trying to arrest him on the street wouldn't work. We'd wanted to do that. We'd been tracking him for a year, waiting for the day we had enough evidence to pick him up. He'd been taking long walks almost every night. We figured it'd be easy to pick him up on any one of those nights. But then, the night we finally got the goods on him, he stopped taking those walks. He hasn't been away from his men since. Somehow, he knows something went wrong. Otherwise, our window wouldn't have closed just when we needed it to stay open.

If I abort now, I know we won't be able to grab him on the street. He'll never be on the street again.

Our next idea was to arrest him at his hotel. For this trip, he and his entourage rented two entire floors and then some at a crappy cinderblock structure in Sunset Park that reviewers had labeled "The Worst Hotel in Brooklyn". The place had become very popular since he'd started staying there. His men man the lobby and the elevator doors on his floor. But his followers occupy pretty much every other room in the place.

We didn't want to create another Waco in the middle of New York City. It would actually be worse than Waco. David Koresh had under a hundred dedicated followers. Aji, the man I'm after, has tens of millions. The cost in violence, FBI budgets and the career paths of high-level bureaucrats ruled this approach clean out of the picture.

It still does.

When we'd felt like we'd run out of options, I'd suggested arresting him at one of his events. It was meant as a joke. I'd claimed that it'd be a way of balancing the PR playing field. If we went in quietly, but in a public place, he wouldn't be able to stop us. It would make *him* look bad to make a scene or to turn out his thugs in force. Somehow, the Special Agent in Charge of the New York field office decided to glom on to *that* idea. It was incredibly risky though. If Aji's guys were good enough, they'd whisk our guys away and those watching would be the none the wiser. Aji's guys might just be good enough. We know they are capable of terrible things.

It was our only option, but it was a damned dangerous option nonetheless.

That's why we decided on a team of six agents. Aji has fifteen thugs – actual former child soldiers – in his inner entourage. Six unarmed, but highly trained, agents aren't enough to look like a massive show of force. But it is enough to cause quite a disturbance even if 15 guys try to quietly disappear them.

As the planning had unfolded in one of the New York field office's sterile conference rooms, I'd thought of *Black Hawk Down*. In order to look peaceful, the US military had down-armored our soldiers in Mogadishu. Predictably, they got slaughtered. I was worried exactly the same thing would happen to us. Six unarmed agents in a huge crowd could find themselves in a whole lot of trouble.

And now? Now, there aren't six of us. Somehow, Aji's guys stopped the other five from getting into the Bandshell Pavilion. We'd planned for one or two guys not making it. If any Agent got turned away, he wouldn't flash his badge or make a scene. We were concerned that if one of us did that, then Aji himself might not even show up at today's event. We were even more concerned that he might stop doing public events altogether. Then, we might be back to invading the fourth floor of a five-story cinderblock hotel in Brooklyn filled with hundreds of devotees of a tremendously popular guru.

We'd be back to Waco, only a million times worse.

Sure, we'd get Aji eventually, but the cost would be very high.

What we hadn't planned on was only one of us getting through. The possibility hadn't crossed our mind. We hadn't decided what to do in that case. Now that I'm alone, nobody would blame me for pulling out. Nonetheless, I have to stay. I have to use this chance. I can't let it slip away. I've got to get this guy because if I don't, I'm not sure anybody else will have the guts to do what needs to be done.

A risky plan has become a stupid one, but I've still got to get through it. So, I do. I spend the next five hours trying to keep my heart rate down by talking to the woman next to me. Her name is Mia. We talk about our lives and our families. I pad a few real elements of my own story with a whole lot of nonsense. I can talk about the Met for days.

Eventually, long after the park is chock full of people, the lights go up on the bandshell.

The crowd's chatter had been growing in volume and excitement. Now, like a candle being blown out, the voices behind me die away in a sudden rush. Two huge screens have been set up on either side of the stage in front of me. Fields of faces flash by in a rush, representing a few hundred of the millions watching the event. And then a Hebrew phrase is projected on one screen, with English, Spanish, Chinese, Tagalog and Vietnamese translations on the other.

It is the Priestly Blessing:

יְבָרֶכְךָ יקוק, וְיִשְׁמְרֶךָ
יָאֵר יקוק פָּנָיו אֵלֶיךָ, וִיחֻנֶּךָּ
יִשָּׂא יקוק פָּנָיו אֵלֶיךָ, וְיָשֵׂם לְךָ שָׁלוֹם

*May the Lord **bless** you and keep You*

May He make His face shine upon you and be gracious to you,
May He lift up His face unto you, and give you peace.

The word *bless* is highlighted, as it always is.

The crowd's silent anticipation grows and then, a moment later, Aji Abakar steps onto the stage. He's a slight man with a close-cut afro, a broad nose and heavy lips. He has no fancy religious garb, just a white cotton shirt and trousers. They contrast sharply with his dark brown skin. I know he's in his early 20s, just a bit younger than me. Nonetheless, he carries a sense of experience with him that suggests a far older man. It's the first time I've seen him in person. An uncontrolled thrill runs through me as I look at him. I remind myself that he uses that charisma to overwhelm the gullible.

Aji's act doesn't follow the preacher's usual script. He doesn't open his arms wide, grin a sh-t-eating grin, and embrace *his* people. He's too good to be *that* obvious.

Instead, the lights from the stage swivel around. They shine on the crowd. I know the camera feed is doing the same. People look up towards the lights, where they know the cameras are. And they smile, sharing how happy they are to be here. I watch Aji himself. As always, he's holding a microphone in his hand. It is an unnecessary object in a world of headsets and sound guns. I wonder if it's real – or if it is some sort of backup weapon.

Then the light shifts and *I'm* in the middle of it. It's like I'm in an interrogation from some old movie. I can't see anything. But I know Aji is looking straight at me. I know the world is. I know the Special Agent in Charge is. He's probably wondering what the hell I'm still doing here.

Then, while the camera is still on me, Aji looks right at me. He seems to pause, as if surprised by something. I see him take a sudden breath. Then, he speaks his first words. His voice is soft and buttery. He has just a hint of a foreign accent – inherited from his immigrant parents. He says, "May the Lord bless you *all*."

His emphasis is on that final word. Like I need a *special* blessing. Like he knows why I'm here. A chill runs down my spine; a stupid plan has become damned near suicidal. At the same time, I want him to say something more.

When the lights shift back to Aji, I find myself embracing the sudden darkness. Mia, sitting next to me, is resting her hand on my arm. *"He blessed you!"* she says in an awestruck whisper.

In the back of my mind I hear myself responding, in a stunned voice, "He blessed me." Mia will think I'm enthralled, not nearly overcome by fear. She won't know I'm freaking out.

The crowd waits, silently. There are no shouts of "Praise the Lord!" or "May G-d bless you!" or anything else. They just sit, ready to listen.

Then Aji begins to speak.

"Last week, we were in Philadelphia. We had the chance to hear the prayers of a few honored people - young and old. I would like to share clips from those heartfelt requests today. Later, we will talk to those same people and see if they have seen any blessing in their lives."

He turns to the screens. A black teenaged boy appears. It's video from the week before. He's on another stage, this one a far larger space in Philadelphia's Fairmont Park. He looks exhausted.

"Aji," the boy says, "I want a car."

"Why?" asks Aji, his gentle voice carrying through the recording.

"I got a special scholarship for talented inner-city kids. I take the bus for three hours every day from West Philly to Chestnut Hill and back. With a car I could save two hours a day. The way things are, I'm afraid I'm gonna need to drop out. I love the school, but it's just too much. So, I'm prayin' for a car."

The video fades away. Another takes its place. This is of an older white man. He looks run down and beat up. His face is grizzled, his skin leathery. "A house," he says, in response to an imaginary question we can't hear.

"Why?" asks Aji, in that same voice.

"Why does anybody want a home? They want someplace to call their own. They want their pride. They want their dignity. That's okay to ask for, right?"

The video fades away. There's another and another and yet another. 5 requests, one after the other. Every week, there are 5 requests.

Barely 5 minutes later, they come to an end.

"We'll talk to these people later," Aji says, "But now I want to talk to you."

The lights refocus on the crowd. As they sweep across it, people raise their hands, eager to speak. Eager to pray. Eager to be blessed. Even Mia has her hands up.

Despite myself, I feel the energy in the crowd.

"You," says Aji, pointing. A man stands up, surprised to be chosen. He walks towards the stage, seeming to grow more and more nervous with each step. When he's finally standing alongside Aji, he's almost shaking.

Aji touches his arm, seeming to calm him.

"What's your name?" he asks.

"Jason... Jason Boyle," the man blurts.

"Okay Jason," says Aji, "Tell us about yourself."

"Uh..." the man is frozen.

"What do you do for a living?" asks Aji.

The man reacts like he's been thrown a life preserver.

"I'm an accountant. I work in Jersey City."

"Big firm? Little place? Little shop in a mall?"

"Uh, a big firm. I actually have a pretty senior position."

"Okay," says Aji, "Where'd you grow up?"

"Upstate. Buffalo."

"You came down here for college."

"Yeah, uh no. I, uh, got a Ph.D. in accounting at Cornell. I came to New York because that's where the best jobs are."

"Okay," says Aji, gently.

"Okay," says the man, girding himself.

"You know what I'm going to ask next?"

"Yes... yes, I know," says the man.

"But you don't want to tell me. You don't want to tell all these people what you're praying for, do you?"

"I'd rather not," says the man.

"It's a good choice, Jason. You know the saying?"

"No," says Jason, "No, I don't."

Aji smiles, warmly. It unnerves me. "Honor, love and happiness are best sought indirectly. If you seek them too eagerly, they'll flee from you."

The man nods, but he doesn't look like he understands.

"We'll talk next week," says Aji.

The man steps down from the stage. And then I realize what his prayer was. He has honor – a good job, a senior position. He wants love, he needs love – and with it, happiness.

The process continues just as I would have expected. Three more people are chosen. We learn a little bit about each of them, we learn and understand what they're seeking.

It would be a wonderful, life-affirming, experience if I didn't know what Aji actually was.

Then the spotlight turns to me.

Out of the thousands of people who are there, the lights turn to me – for the second time that night.

My hands aren't up. Mia's are. But mine aren't.

This is not coincidence.

"Your turn," says Aji. His voice is inviting, enticing, welcoming. Like he's saving these words especially for me.

"My blessing has already been granted," I say. The sound gun picks up my voice and broadcasts it around the world.

"Your turn," insists Aji.

I imagine the Special Agent in Charge watching me walk up to the stage. My legs feel like jelly.

I don't have a prayer.

"What's your name?" Aji asks.

"Alison," I say.

"Alison," he repeats, slowly, as if he knows I'm making it up. "Alison, where are you from?"

"L.A."

"Why'd you come here?"

"An opportunity," I say, "I work for the Met. I'm a curator."

I don't know how well the lie will work when millions are watching. Certainly, somebody at the Met will know I don't work there. I don't know what else to do, though.

Aji says, "You were blessed, and that's why you came here?"

Damned, I forgotten the key word. I say, "Yes, I was blessed."

Aji nods. "And now you have a prayer?"

"No, no," I say, "My prayers have been answered."

"You have a prayer," he says again. This time, it isn't a question.

I scramble for something. But I don't know what Alison who works at the Met would want. I blurt out, without thinking, "I want those who are evil to be stopped."

Aji doesn't flinch. "That's an unusual prayer for an Alison who works at the Met. More importantly, it's a very general *thought* – like asking for world peace. It isn't *your* prayer. I want *your* prayer. I want to know what *you* want."

The lights are on me. The crowd is watching. The cameras are capturing every moment. I can't think of anything else. I can't put myself in Alison's shoes. I imagine my heart rate is so high the radio in my upper arm is making the cameras flicker. I need *something*.

I almost shout out, "*I* want to stop those who are evil!"

Aji says, "Now *that* is a prayer. We'll hear from you next week."

One way or another, I know that isn't happening.

I walk off the stage, as coolly as I can manage. I take my seat next to Mia, the Latina woman with the baby. She's smiling at me, glowing. But I'm shaking.

What kind of game was Aji playing?

And what the heck is going to happen now?

"Let's revisit our prayers from last week." says Aji.

A face appears on the big screen. It is the young man who wanted a car. He's live on some video conferencing system.

"What has happened in the last week?" asks Aji, "Did you get your car?"

"No," says the teenager. His face is glowing though. The exhaustion from the previous week is gone. There's an energy in him now.

"Something happened though," says Aji. It is a statement, not a question.

"I met someone, on the bus."

"A girl?" asks Aji.

"No," says the boy, "A kid. He rides the bus a couple times a week, in the morning. His dad lives in West Philly. His mom in Germantown. They have joint custody, but no car. He's only 10 and so his dad brings him up to his mom on the way to his job in Chestnut Hill."

"Okay," says Aji.

"Well, the kid is struggling in school. With math. But he really wants to do well."

"Where do you come in?" asks Aji.

"Well, I can help him. I'm only 16 and *I* can help him because I'm going to that elite school. Oh, and because I'm on that bus. Three times a week, while ridin' on the bus, I'm tutoring him. And I'm gonna change his life."

Aji smiles. He turns from the screen and back to the crowd.

"That," he says, "is the core of blessing. A blessing isn't a thing. It isn't money or power or health or a car. A blessing is an opportunity, and it can come in any form. And the greatest opportunity is the opportunity to bless others."

"Amen," says the teenager in the video. For the first time, the crowd utters something. An "amen" ripples through it.

The screen changes. The older man is there now. The one who'd been praying for a home. This man is also smiling. He's shaved – at least as well as he could, given his leathery skin.

"Has anything happened in your life?" asks Aji.

14

"Yes," says the man.

"Did you find a home."

"I did," says the man.

"An apartment? A room?" asks Aji.

"No," says the man, "The homeless shelter."

He's bursting, eager to share.

"You're living in the homeless shelter, but you found a home?"

"Yeah," says the man, "A new position opened up. They needed a night manager for the shelter. When I was younger, I used to manage a motel. I told them that. And they hired me. The job comes with a private room, but I'm not even gonna use it."

"Why not?"

"It's what I said last week. I wanted a home, so I'd have someplace to call my own. I wanted a home, so I'd have pride and dignity. I didn't even have to move – and I've got all of that!"

"You found something more important than dignity then. You found purpose." says Aji.

"Yeah, I guess I did," says the man, his smile somehow growing bigger. "I'm staying with the men because I want to be there to help them out."

Again, Aji turns to the crowd.

"Pride and dignity don't come from the material things we have. They come from the purpose we've discovered. We're all here for a reason, we just have to let ourselves find it."

"Amen," says the man.

"Amen," echoes the crowd.

The process continues. One through five. Prayers answered, in unexpected ways. Amens flowing through the crowd.

Then Aji gets to the core of his presentation.

"As I said earlier, blessings are not about physical goods. Blessings are about opportunity. Yes, physical goods matter. They are the fabric on which everything else is built. So I welcome your charitable gifts to my ministry. Far more important than cash is the mission itself. Share the blessings of the Lord. Share my message. Bless me in *that* way and you, in turn, will be blessed."

15

I've seen him say it before. It is remarkably clever. Money is just a currency. A currency that can be traced. Like a Mafioso who trades in favors, Aji knows that you can build influence and power without relying on cash.

We, the FBI, have had a hell of a time trying to trace his trail of influence. Now, though, we've got him.

The televised show draws to a close. The act isn't over, though. In a rush, people move towards the stage – eager to talk one-on-one with Aji Abakar. They are eager to be blessed.

Aji steps down from the stage. Minders appear on either side of him, huge African men with dangerous eyes. Legs shaking, I join the line. I'm about the twentieth person. That's why I got here early, so I'd be sure have a chance to see him one-on-one. That was how I was supposed to make the arrest. Get close, show my badge, and arrest him. My five backups would ensure things wouldn't go too wrong.

Somehow, despite the lack of five backups, my plan hasn't changed. I shuffle forward, feeling the stares of the minders on me. But I keep going.

I'm alone. They've disappeared my team. I know they can make *me* vanish – at least long enough to quietly add me to the Wall of Honor.

Nonetheless, I keep going.

The woman in front of me finishes her brief conversation with Aji. She is guided off to the right by a young lady. It is my turn to step forward. I'm visibly shaking as I step up in front of Aji.

Aji smiles as I step up. He seems truly happy to see me. Then he says, "Special Agent Niesha Jackson."

I freeze. Now I know, for certain, that he knows I'm not Alison.

"Don't be frightened," he says, "I'd just like to do this quietly."

"Do what quietly?" I ask. Is he threatening me?

"You're here to arrest me for the murder of John Buckner, right?"

"Yes," I say, by now only moderately surprised that he knows.

"I'd like you to do that quietly. After these people leave."

I stare at him, wondering if there's some sort of trick. I know I can't exactly shackle him and guide him out through *this* crowd. I'd

16

never make it to the fences. I also know that once these people leave, the area outside the fences will be dominated by *my* people. Without human shields, Aji Abakar will no longer hold all the cards.

I nod my agreement and the young woman guides me off to the right. Rather than leaving, I stand there. I watch as Aji talks to his hundreds of supplicants. I remember my childhood Bible classes and the story of Jethro. Moses would stand from dawn to dusk, judging his people. But this man is no Moses.

It occurs to me that he could still take me hostage. Once the crowds are gone. Scenarios run through my head. But something in me dismisses them as unnecessary fabrications. Some voice tells me that this man will go quietly.

It is after midnight by the time the crowds are gone.

By the time I step forward again, a cool evening breeze is flowing through the park. I decide against the handcuffs. Instead, I take his arm. A little buzz runs through me. I tell myself it is simply the excitement of arresting this man after all this time. "Aji Abakar," I say, "You are under arrest for the murder of John Buckner. You have a right to remain silent. Anything you say can and will be used against you in a court of law. You have a right to an attorney. If you cannot afford an attorney, one will be appointed for you."

Then, as his minders watch my every move, I guide Aji Abakar to the tall fences.

An FBI Suburban, and a small army of men, are waiting for us.

Aji steps inside the SUV, calm and smiling and without any sort of resistance. I sit down next to him, our legs just touching. I force myself to remember, that no matter how charismatic the man is, I'm sitting next to a killer. We drive off towards the FBI Field Office in Lower Manhattan.

First, he disappeared my agents, then he questioned me in front of millions. After all that, he came quietly and without resistance.

I can't figure out what kind of game he thinks he's playing.

Hostage

Monday – 1:03 AM

All of us have pulled our chairs up behind Matthew Crass' desk. "All of us" comprises of five Special Agents and Crass. Crass isn't a Special Agent, he's just a computer genius. The FBI somehow managed to recruit him despite the monetary attractions of Silicon Valley or Wall Street. You know he's a computer genius because it's one o'clock on a Monday morning and he's the only person who doesn't seem either tired or like he's about to OD on caffeine.

Crass' natural home is behind a screen, churning through terabytes of data and unknotting a complex money laundering investigation. That's not what we're doing now. Instead, all of us are watching a pinwheel on one of his many monitors. The system for matching prints, the Next Generation Identification system (or NGI for short) is pretty fast. It was "next generation" in 2010. Just like with the 737NG, the Next Generation thing stuck far longer than it actually had any right to. The system took minutes to run a print. Minutes isn't long, but when you're looking for confirmation of a year's hard work, a few minutes can feel like forever.

As soon as we'd brought Aji Abakar into the Jacob K. Javits Federal Building, we'd taken him up to the 23rd floor, our floor, and booked him. Photographs, essential data, bank account information, the whole nine yards. We knew all that information, of course. What we hadn't had before was his biometric data. We'd needed probable cause to get that. The testimony of the guy he paid to kill John Buckner gave us the probable cause. That man, a transient *actually* named Elvis Brown, claimed Aji Abakar had approached him in a dark alley and offered him $1000 in cash to kill John Buckner. As Elvis might not have passed a psychological examination, his testimony would not have been enough to *convict* Aji. It was enough to arrest him though. We were hoping the biometrics – Aji's fingerprints and DNA – would get us across the line.

The DNA will take a few days to process, even though this is a seriously high-priority case. But the fingerprints can be run immediately. That's why my entire team is sitting watching a pinwheel on Crass' screen. We're all watching as the FBIs 'Next Generation' computer systems slowly compares the prints we just got off of Aji Abakar with the library of physical evidence from a series of thirty-one suspicious deaths and hundreds of possible assaults we suspect Aji Abakar has directed. The system is fastest when you're comparing perfect prints to perfect prints. That's not what we have. We're comparing perfect prints to a broad range of imperfect prints taken from all sorts of crime scenes – no two sets of which seemed to match.

It's only going to be a few minutes, but even Crass looks like he's getting tired.

While we sit there, five pairs of eyes eagerly awaiting our confirmation, my phone keeps going off. I'm getting short little messages: "Congratulations", "Wow", "What a coup!" and so on. Everybody's acting like we brought down John Gotti.

Even people I know outside the FBI are texting me. "Hey, Allison 😊" or "Nice turn on the Abakar show!"

My team doesn't congratulate me, though. Even though I'm remarkably young to be leading a task force, I've earned their respect. They know we haven't got Aji yet and they know that Aji isn't even my target. I want Aji *and* his entire organization.

Because I'm not about to celebrate, they aren't either. Not yet. Instead, our hearts to stop each time the pinwheel shakes or pauses.

My phone vibrates again.

This time, I don't bother checking it.

"Anybody want coffee?" I ask. Nobody says anything.

I'm hoping that as soon as I walk away, the computer will "bing" and we'll get our result. I stand up and make my way towards the lunchroom. But I don't hear a "bing". It doesn't matter. The fact is, I need the coffee anyway. I'm exhausted. I burned through my adrenaline at the park and I'm going to need something else to keep myself going.

I pop my cup under the machine and slot in one of the off-brand pods the FBI is willing to pay for. Then I hit the little coffee button. As the dark liquid splutters out, I wonder how we're going to use what we find.

The prayer I uttered on that stage was real: "I want to stop those who are evil." The question always is: how do I get there from here?

My phone keeps vibrating.

The coffee stops spluttering, and I pick up my cup and begin to head back towards the others. That's when I hear the "bing" of the computer. A millisecond later, I hear the shouts of excitement – "WE GOT A HIT!"

I rush towards the group, as fast as I can manage without spilling anything. The carpet is an anonymous shade of industrial brown for a reason, but I don't have to make it worse.

They all look towards me and then usher me forward and towards the monitor. Nobody says a thing. They're waiting for me to see it. And then I do. At the top of the screen is the rendering of the tenprints – the perfect set of fingerprints taken at booking. There's also a little table at the bottom of the screen.

"Record ID" is one header, "Score" is another. Below it are two lines. The first is the record we just created at booking. The second is *another* record. The first record has a score of 100, it matches itself perfectly. The next line is what's important. I look at the score. It is a 95. It may not be enough for a conviction, but it is certainly enough to push things forward.

If it came from someplace useful.

I grab the mouse and click on the second line. A blown-up set of three prints joins the tenprints at the top of screen. Little yellow streaks and red dots indicate points of comparison. I click on another link to open the description of the record.

And there I see it:

CASE ID: 1217954235

CASE NAME: John Buckner (Murder of)

EVIDENCE ID: 4537795478922

EVIDENCE SOURCE: Elvis Brown

EVIDENCE TYPE: US $5 Bill

The people around me let out an involuntary "whoop!" We haven't won the war, but this is a mighty fine step forward.

Normally, prints can't be lifted off of cash – the material is too absorbent. We'd gone the extra mile though. As soon as the killer said he was paid in cash, the head of our Field Office suggested we ask the FBI Laboratory if they had something that could help. They told us not to handle the money any more than absolutely necessary. Then they sent down a special portable laser scanner and every bill was scanned in situ. Dozens of usable prints were turned up. We ran them all. The killer had a few and a few other known individuals had some too. But most were unknown.

Now, we can recognize one of those unknown prints. Aji Abakar's prints were on the money.

We have what need to keep moving forward: Aji handled the cash that Elvis Brown claimed he was paid. And Elvis Brown definitely killed John Buckner.

My phone is still buzzing.

I know we'll need confirmation by a fingerprint technician. We might even get some DNA that would further strengthen the case. But what we have is enough to get started. I drain my coffee, shoot up from my chair and begin to head towards the interrogation rooms. The team follows behind him. It is time to push Aji further and leverage what we've got to shut him *and* his crew down.

Just then, my phone starts ringing.

I pull it from my pocket and see that the Special Agent in Charge (or SAC) James Miller, is calling. The SAC runs the Field Office. In Miller's case, it is the New York Field Office, the most important in the nation. SAC Millar probably wants to congratulate me too. And maybe himself along the way. After all, he recruited me from my dead-end job in California. He put me in charge of this task force. I owe him. I hit the green button and put the phone to my ear.

"Where are you?" he asks.

"About to interrogate the prisoner." I say.

"I've been texting you frantically. We need you in Conference Room 3."

"Why?"

"Neisha, the Director of the FBI is here. She's waiting for *you*."

"I'll be there in a minute," I say. I hang up and slide the phone back into my pocket.

The Director, Sheila Markoff, is the first woman to head the Bureau. She looks the part of a perfect senior law enforcement officer. She's fit and lean with dark hair, brown eyes and slightly browned skin. She looks like an older version of a Special Agent from a movie. The rumors in the agency is that she was picked because she combined a reasonably credible career history with perfect optics.

Respect for her does not run high.

Of course, respect and respectfulness are two different things. She is considered a political wizard and so nobody is eager to get on her bad side. I may not want to talk to the Director, but I don't exactly get to ignore her summons.

"I'll meet you there," I tell the team. Then I veer off towards the conference room.

As I push open the heavy door into the secure, windowless space, I see three faces turn to look at me. Only one, SAC Miller, is actually in the room. The other two are only there by video conference.

I don't feel as bad about ignoring my phone.

"Any updates?" asks SAC Miller, expectantly. SAC Miller has a well-defined face, a solid jaw, piercing blue eyes and the pepper gray hair of a man with experience and more than a bit of wisdom. He seems almost like a President or a Senator, perfectly packaged and wholly confident in his own capabilities. With the exception of the blue eyes, I sometimes like to imagine myself in his position.

"Yes, sir," I say, "We got a fingerprint match on the money Elvis Brown said he was paid."

SAC Miller does a little celebratory fist pump – like he just won a tennis set. I think I'd be a little more expressive, if I were in his position.

"We got the bastard," he says. He continues, half to me and half to the people on the video call, "I just have to say, that was an incredibly gutsy arrest. We were all watching remotely. You kept up that conversation with that woman next to you – cool as a cucumber. You went on stage and got through that. And then you just walked up and arrested the man. It was incredible. It was a real testament to the quality of the New York Field Office."

SAC Miller is no political slouch. With a few sentences, he managed to use me to make his entire office look good in front of the Director of the FBI.

I don't join in the congratulations, though. It all misses the point. The evidence isn't there just to "get the guy." I want to use the evidence to get "all the guys."

The Director looks out from the monitor and asks, "So how do we play this?"

I have my answer. I am by far the most junior person in the room, though. So, I don't say anything.

The third person 'here' via videoconference does. He is a polished looking middle-aged man with just a hint of gray hair.

"In case Special Agent Jackson doesn't know me," he says, "I am the Assistant Director of the Office of Public Affairs. I want to lay out the basics of the situation. The simple issue is this: Aji Abakar is a wildly popular spiritual guide. Remarkably, he is popular among both Christians *and* Jews. He even has Muslim followers and quite a few non-religious folks who've been attracted to his message. When we charge him, the agency will run the risk of being seen as *anti-religious,* not *anti-crime.* He can, and almost certainly will, cast himself as a martyr. For all sorts of reasons, we need to mitigate that."

"All sorts of reasons" is a euphemism for political careers and Bureau budgets. I haven't been around long, but I still understand that.

SAC Miller jumps in. "You are absolutely right, Roger. To me the answer is simple. We need to throw everything at him. Show the evidence to the public, show the pattern to the public and let the public condemn him as the dangerous charlatan he is. *And,* we need do it fast. We don't want *his* camp framing the story. Somehow they'll make him look like the innocent victim of D.C.-based persecution."

I clear my voice. I may be a minnow in this crowd, but I care about this case. The three senior operatives' faces turn towards me. I'm still standing by the door.

"Director, if I may. We have an opportunity here."

"What opportunity?" asks the Director. She seems relieved to have something other than risks to think about.

"We seem so focused on Aji Abakar, but we actually have a chance to bring his whole organization down."

"That doesn't change how we handle the public," says Roger Cox.

"It may," I say, "Aji said he wanted things done quietly. And – "

SAC Miller cuts me off, "*He's* a criminal, we're the FBI. He doesn't call the shots."

"Oh, I know," I say, "But he *wants* things done quietly. That means we have a hostage."

The room is silent. Nobody is willing to admit they have no idea what I'm talking about.

I continue, "So long as we haven't gone public, we can *threaten* to go public."

The faces are still blank.

Maybe they need a little more context. I say, "We suspect Aji's involvement in 31 separate deaths. We got him on one. Just one. And none of his team were implicated. There's a network here. A dangerous network. If we get rid of him, one of his lieutenants might take over what we know is a lucrative and powerful operation. We'll be back where we were a year ago with a whole new guy who might not make the same kind of mistakes. This is the chance to bring the whole thing down. We can work with Aji to minimize *his* role, so far as the public is concerned. In return, he can give us *his* people."

"Why would he do that?" asks the Director.

"Because the man is obsessed with his image. He's always implying that people should bless him. He has a track-record, although we can't prove it, of *murdering* his critics. If we agree to hold off on arraigning him, and then ask the judge to keep things under seal until trial, we might be able to get him to cooperate. We could even take it further and publicly blame what has happened on his overly aggressive deputies while charging him with murder nonetheless."

"But if his people talk first, they'll control the story," says SAC Miller.

"Have they talked?" I ask.

"No," says the Roger Cox, "They haven't released any information."

"They knew I was coming. If the plan was to talk, they would have had a press release ready to go. Aji *wants* quiet. As soon as we mouth off, we lose the single biggest piece of leverage we have."

SAC Miller doesn't look like he agrees. Nonetheless, he turns towards the Director. She's going to make the call.

"I agree with Special Agent Jackson," she says, after a moment's consideration. "We don't want Aji's cancer to spread just because we failed to cut out the entire tumor."

"But Special Agent Jackson," she adds, "Keep in mind your position in the FBI. You've earned the right to call some shots here, but that comes with risk. If this goes well, you're on the podium when we make the other arrests. You get the boost. You could have an incredible future with the Bureau. But if it goes wrong – if the FBI looks bad – nobody will ever know what you pulled off today. You understand?"

I nod towards the camera. "Yes, ma'am," I say.

I care about stopping the bad guys and I know this is the best way to do it.

"Can I go now?" I ask.

"Yes," she announces.

I turn around, open the door again and walk out. Behind me, the discussion continues although I have no idea what else there is to discuss.

As I charge down the coffee-brown hallway towards Interrogation 2, my thoughts are focused on Aji Abakar.

My prisoner is waiting.

Threat

Monday – 1:29 AM

I stop in at the observation room before going in to interrogate Aji. In theory, I just want to get a sense of his mental state and prepare myself for the interrogation. In reality, I want to ask Clara McGuinness whether *she'd* handle the interview. I am worried Aji will somehow overwhelm me. Clara is in her late 40s and has almost 20 years of experience under her belt. She's seen every move a suspect could try to pull; nothing seems to faze her. I've only been an agent for a year and half, and I am not sure I'm up to interrogating someone of this caliber.

Clara's answer? "Neisha, you're going to have to learn how to do this. You might as well start now."

I know that, of course. Just like a surgeon has to practice on people they don't want dying, an FBI agent has to practice on people they don't want getting away. I don't want to learn with Aji, though. I just want to put him and his crew away. Something about him, and the hypocrisy of what he has done, seriously pisses me off.

These are the thoughts that are going through my head as I push open the door to the interrogation room itself. I have the case file, thick with papers, under my arm.

Aji looks up and smiles broadly as I enter. He is still wearing his white cotton trousers and shirt. His arms, though, are shackled to the table.

"I'm glad to see you, Neisha." His eyes seem to sparkle with some unexplained pleasure. I ignore his greeting. The light is harsh in this room, all high-power UV and nothing soft or inviting.

I get right to it.

"As I told you when you were arrested, you have a right to counsel. Do you have a lawyer you would like to contact prior to this interview?"

"You can ask me anything you'd like, Neisha. I don't need a lawyer," he answers.

I'm surprised. A lawyer is a very good idea when dealing with the FBI. Lying to a Federal Officer is a Federal offense. Eventually, in an extensive interview, everybody either lies about something or screws something up. That alone can be enough to send you to prison.

Nonetheless, I've asked. I've given him the chance to lawyer up. It's not my fault that he, with all his resources, hasn't summoned someone top-notch. Maybe he's hoping his personality will get him through this.

"Okay," I say. "Let's get started."

I'm about the wipe the smile off his face.

"Do you know the story of Al Capone?" I ask.

"No," says Aji.

"He was a mobster in the 1920s. He covered his tracks, almost perfectly. They couldn't get him on murder or bootlegging. But he was suspected in the murders of hundreds of people. Eventually, they got him on tax evasion."

"Why are you telling me this?" asks Aji. He looks worried. I feel a little thrill of triumph.

"Aji, I know you've killed dozens of people," I say.

"What?" he asks. Suddenly, Aji's face seems overcome by shock. The reaction is stronger than I'd expected. Pretending to be surprised won't get him out of this.

I ignore him and continue, "But you're very good at covering your tracks. In your case, though, we aren't going to do what we did to Capone. Because we finally caught you red-handed. You're going away for life."

"Dozens?" he asks, seemingly not caring about John Buckner.

I push ahead.

"John Buckner was an internet blogger who criticized you continually. He said you were a charlatan, a fake, a criminal. You know all this, don't you?"

"Yes," he says, in a wavering voice.

"John Buckner's house suffered a gas leak three weeks ago. It exploded shortly thereafter. Because of the pattern of violence against those who criticize you, we immediately looked into it. We found

27

video footage of a transient white male leaving the property. We found him and interrogated him. He claimed that you paid him to blow up the house."

Aji just looks at me, his expression serious.

"Today, we ran your fingerprints. We found *your* fingerprints on cash in the transient male's possession. It is clear you paid him. We're going to charge you for the murder of John Buckner."

Aji looks at me. He seems *worried* about me.

"Neisha —" he says.

I cut him off.

"I am *Special Agent Jackson*. We aren't friends."

His hands pull up against the shackles like he's trying to wave them in submission. "Special Agent Jackson, I think you're a remarkable person."

"I don't care what you think." I say.

"Special Agent Jackson, *please* tread carefully. I don't want you to get hurt, or worse."

It takes me a moment to realize what he's doing.

"Are you threatening me?"

"No, no," he says, his eyes seeming to plead, "I'm *praying* for you."

I look into his eyes then and I see care and compassion. Like he actually *believes* he's praying for me. I'm almost drawn in. I almost feel like I want to protect him because *he* wants to protect me. The control he shows is chilling. I can't let him take control of the interview.

"We can keep this quiet," I suggest, trying to get back to my original plan.

"That would be best," he says.

"In return, you can tell us how it all works."

"I'll tell you how it works, even if you don't keep it quiet. It's simple: G-d blesses those who bless me, and curses those who curse me."

I know the verse. It is from the Bible. G-d promises Abraham He will bless those who bless him and curse those who curse him.

It is nonsensical. I'm happy about the distance it puts between me and him.

Aji isn't done. "Don't curse me, Special Agent Jackson. I don't want *you* to be cursed. Instead, arrange to release me under my own recognizance. Then, we'll work this out in the most positive way possible."

I can't believe what I'm hearing. I feel anger beginning to boil up within me.

"You do realize I'm an FBI agent. You can't threaten me. I have the power of the Federal Government behind me."

"I'm not threatening you," he says, "But you're dealing with a force you can't understand, much less challenge."

His confidence is unsettling. It might even be justified. Aji's people found the other 5 FBI agents. They probably knew who they were. Aji knew who I was, even as he interviewed "Alison" the curator in front of millions of people. Aji knew when the FBI got its arrest warrant, which is why he stopped going out by himself the same night we had the evidence we needed.

I want to get claws into his organization, but after a year of trying, I don't have any. At least, none that have led anywhere. But Aji has claws in mine.

In that moment, I realize I've lost control of the entire situation. I arrested Aji, but he let me do it. The man sitting in front of me is dictating *everything* that happens. And his network is far deeper that I'd even imagined it could be. He's willing to kill, he knows everything I know, and now he's warning me to tread carefully. One of my team members, on a special FBI task force, might even be working for him.

He's toying with me. I'm shaking as I stand up.

"Are you okay?" he asks, that same frightening concern in his voice. I don't answer, I just pick up the case file.

"One more thing," he says, "It's about your brother."

I turn to him, shocked.

"I just want you to know that I believe G-d has a plan."

I almost stumble out of the room.

Protection

Monday – 1:43 AM

When I close the door of the interview room behind me, it gives a satisfying and solid clunk. Aji won't be leaving. His *energy* will be contained. Clara is waiting for me. She lays her arm over my shoulder, reassuringly.

"It's okay, Neisha" she says, "You did fine."

I expected to feel safe, coming out of the interrogation room. But even with the door between us, I don't feel safe. Instead, I look at Clara, suddenly worried that she might be one of Aji's plants. I can't tell. I have no way of knowing. I have no idea who I can trust.

Clara keeps talking. "I've already told SAC Miller about the interview. He's coming over now."

A moment later, I see James Miller barreling down the hallway. "Did he threaten you?" Miller asks, as soon as he reaches me.

"It's all on the tapes," says Clara. I tell myself that she can't be a plant if she's explaining things to Miller, right?

The problem is, I just don't know.

"They do that sometimes," says Miller, "but you don't have to worry. He's locked up. I can go have a chat with him and remind him of his place in the world if you'd like."

"I think he knows his place better than we do," says Clara. "I watched the interview. Neisha didn't screw it up. He just took over. I think he knows more about us than we know about him."

I add, "It almost feels like being locked up is part of *his* plan."

Miller pauses to think. "Okay, it's been a very long day. Very challenging. Let's take some time out and revisit this in the morning. Neisha, do you feel like there's an actual threat to your safety?"

I don't want to look like I am frightened. But I am. I'm scared of Clara. I'm scared of SAC Miller. I'm scared of some other agent or janitor or – who knows what – waiting to punish me for not treading carefully. Will Aji try to do anything to me if *I* haven't done anything yet? Then again, I have done something. I arrested him.

Clara jumps in, "There is a credible threat, sir. Not only that, but the man clearly has resources inside the FBI. I'm not sure *we* can protect Neisha."

"Really?" asks SAC Miller. The disbelief is written all over his face.

"Sir, he's probably killed over 30 people and we haven't caught him. He has an active network. He knew who our guys were. He told Neisha to tread carefully for her own sake. He knew she was going to arrest him. He's a *real* threat."

Reluctantly, SAC Miller nods his head. "Okay. The US Marshalls are a block from here. I'll ask them to cover you for the night."

"Thanks," I say. I don't want to show my relief, but I feel it. Clara and SAC Miller have got to be okay, right? There's no way either one is setting up with some crooked US Marshalls, is there?

It is disconcerting, not knowing who is truly on your side.

A pair of US Marshalls arrive 15 minutes later. I hear the ding of the elevator and then see them round the corner from reception. They're wearing blue tee-shirts and light khaki pants. Covering these innocuous-looking clothes are bulletproof vests, utility belts and pistol holsters flamboyantly strapped to their thighs. Silver stars hang from chains around their necks. The two US Marshalls aren't huge, but they look like they are ready for violence.

I don't know them. Then again, I don't *really* know anybody.

I stick out my hand as they approach, "Special Agent Jackson."

I want to reinforce my status as a Federal Agent. After all, these guys could take me anywhere they want to, and they could do anything they want when they get there.

In turn, they murmur politely, and introduce themselves. Each one shakes my hand.

Then, we turn and walk to the elevators.

As they guide me through the garage, I watch them warily. I don't want to insult them, but I'm as jumpy as I've ever been. I find myself worried about being trapped when they help me into the back of an armored SUV.

Even then, I don't relax. I pull my Glock from its holster and hold it in my lap. No matter what's coming, I'm going to put up a fight. If the US Marshalls notice what I've done, they don't say anything. Instead, the lumbering vehicle pulls out of the driveway and on to Duane Street. A few moments later, we bounce over the tips of the bollards that guard each end of the Federal Plaza.

As we turn north, one question fills my mind. Everything in the interview made sense, given what I know about Aji Abakar.

One thing didn't: Why had Aji decided to mention my brother?

Something inside feels like that question is the key to everything.

Killing

Monday – 2:12 AM

I grew up in a place that looked like a completely normal lower-middle-class neighborhood. People lived in small houses. They weren't that well maintained, but there were cars on the street and a decent majority ran just fine. There were kids who played. There were schools and even playgrounds. There were sidewalks with kid's bicycles strewn on them.

At first glance, it would seem like a perfectly decent place to grow up.

It wasn't.

Some people have an early memory of opening a present, walking in some park or holding their mother's hand. My first memories are of a feeling: fear. It was constant. It was everywhere. You'd walk down the street aware that there could be shooting at any moment. There were robberies, drug deals and fights. You learned, instinctively, to rely on your fear to keep you safe. You learned to recognize danger that an outsider would never even see.

I grew up on the South Side of Chicago and I hated it.

My mother had grown up in South Side. She'd been the daughter of a teenage mother. She'd made some mistakes of her own; I was one. Then she'd put herself through Community College as a single mom and she'd gotten a job. Slowly but surely, she'd risen the ranks. She wasn't some high-flyin' executive. What she was was the branch manager of a pharmacy in Chicago's fancy Loop neighborhood. It was a decent job. It was enough for us to move out of the South Side. We didn't move though.

I used to beg her to move. I used to beg her to move us someplace safe. She wouldn't do it. When I was eleven, I got tired of asking. While she was at work one Sunday, I took my little brother, LaMarcus, and we walked over to the G-d's Miracle Baptist Church. My mom would swear by the pastor of that church, our church. She had that very morning. I figured that I'd just talk to him, explain things to him, and we'd be out of the South Side in a jiffy.

That afternoon, I showed up at the Church and I knocked on the pastor's office door. When he opened it, I took LaMarcus's hand and we strode right on in.

He looked at the two of us. I looked at him. Then I said to him, "Pastor, my momma makes enough money to move out of here. It ain't safe here. You gotta tell her to go."

He looked right down at me. He didn't chuckle. He didn't comment on how cute, or brave, I was. He just asked me to sit down on his beat-up old couch. Then he sat down behind his desk and he said, "Neisha, your mom *wants* to move."

I didn't know that. It shocked me. "Then why don't she?" I asked.

"Because I asked her not to."

I just stared at him. What business would a pastor have telling a mom with two young kids to stay in a place like this? I was mad at him. I remember that. But he had an answer.

"Neisha," he said, "If a place like this is gonna have any hope, it's got to be built around pillars of the community. Your mom is a pillar of this community. She shows people how things could be better. Judging by how you walked in here today, I think *you* will be a pillar of the community. You gotta do what you can to raise people up. Then you gotta rely on G-d to take care of the rest."

My 11-year-old ears heard one message: I didn't have to worry. I could be safe. G-d was gonna' take care of us because we were pillars of our community.

He was the pastor and I *believed* him.

The pastor offered me a ride home. But I didn't take it. I was full of pride. I wasn't gonna lean on him. Soon enough, he was gonna be the one leanin' on me. As I walked out of that church, LaMarcus holding my hand, I felt like I was protecting him, and G-d was protecting me.

For the first time in my life, I felt safe.

I felt safe as I walked past the car with the idling engine and the four young men sitting in it. I felt safe as I walked us towards the house with the too-loud party. I felt safe when I heard the car rev its engine behind us.

It was already too late when I realized that G-d wasn't gonna take care of us. I shoved LaMarcus down just as the bullets came flying out of the side of that car. The people in the house were ready. They fired back. LaMarcus and I were caught in the middle.

I wasn't hit. It was a miracle.

LaMarcus was hit once. In the head.

He never even had a chance to say goodbye.

My mother never spoke to me again. For the years I remained in her house, we lived silently – like two ghosts inhabiting a shared space. My mother was silent, but LaMarcus wasn't. He'd come to me in my dreams and he'd ask the same question every time: "Why?"

Aji Abakar had brought up my brother. But I can't understand why. It couldn't have been a demonstration of his willingness to use violence. Aji was only six when my brother was killed. He wasn't driving that car or holding the gun. And he grew up in LA, not Chicago.

Was he trying to scare me by showing how much he knew about my background? It was possible. But a public records search would have uncovered the story. If he knew I was coming for him, it wasn't that surprising that he'd know about LaMarcus.

Maybe he was warning me that he is only part of an older and bigger network? That possibility was truly frightening. But that network wouldn't have targeted an eight-year-old boy and his eleven-year-old sister. There couldn't be a connection.

As the armored SUV pulls up to my building at 139th and Lenox – in the heart of Harlem – I can only think of one answer.

For some twisted reason, Aji Abakar was trying to mess with my head.

As the US Marshalls guide me into my building, I imagine I can hear little LaMarcus asking: "Why?"

Smoke

Monday – 4:23 AM

I hear a pounding. It is insistent, dangerous, repeated. Again, and again, like rounds shot out by a cannon– WHAM! WHAM! I'm on a street. I turn, look down and see LaMarcus. He's looking at me, screaming in terror. And he's hitting me. His arms pound into me, but I don't feel anything. But I hear it, his arms flail against me and with every strike there is a boom like gunfire.

I wake up, screaming.

I wake up in total darkness. The room is hot. And everything is silent but the pounding. I'm confused for a moment. I don't know where I am. There's a smell in the air. Acrid. Sour. A moment later I see it. There's a cloud in the room, a dark cloud of smoke hovering in the air. There are no lamps I can see. No illumination from the city outside. Instead there is just smoke, like a blanket slowly being lowered over me.

I'm home. I'm home. And my home is on fire. I scramble off the bed. The floor is hot, very hot, but the air is clearer there. I gasp for something, my lungs burn. I hear the pounding. WHAM! WHAM! WHAM! Then I realize what it must be. The US Marshalls brought me here, to my apartment. I wouldn't let them inside. I didn't trust them. I trusted my door, with its deadbolts and crossbars, to keep me safe.

Now that same door may condemn me.

I can't remember which way I'm facing. But I can hear that pounding. I scramble across the hot floor. My hands smoke as they touch the surface. I scream in pain but keep pushing forward. I can't afford to stop. WHAM! WHAM! WHAM!

I see it now, the bottom of my door. I draw in one hot breath and then kneel, keeping my head close to the ground. I tear my shirt off over my head. I wrap it around my hands. And I reach up. How many locks are there? I try to remember. Three. There are three locks. WHAM! WHAM! WHAM!

First the cross bolt. There are two steel bars that reach across the door. I have to twist a lever in the middle and they'll retract. I reach out desperately, trying to find the lever in the dark and the heat.

My hands, burned from touching the ground, are in unbelievable pain. All I can think about is the pain. Then I feel the lever. I grab it. Somehow, I know that my shirt, wrapped around my hand, is in flames. The steel is just too hot. I pull the lever. The crossbars retreat.

I scream and fall back to the ground. The pain is too much. Two more locks. I have to undo two more locks.

That's my last thought before everything goes dark.

When I begin to open my eyes, I can feel that I'm outside. There's fresh air around me. I'm on something uncomfortable. I'm bouncing. I must be on a gurney. I can make out the dim shape of a US Marshall's uniform above me and to the right. Another man is hovering over my left.

"She's coming to!" the man says. My vision clears some more, and I see the man is in a paramedic's uniform.

The US Marshall is hovering over me. His face covered in soot and his hair is singed. I see bandages on his hands. He must have been the one who'd been banging on my door. He must have broken through my locks after I'd opened the cross bolt.

I mumble something. I want to know what happened. I try to move. Almost immediately, I'm hit by a wave of nausea. I turn to the side and vomit. The feel of it screams up my throat. The US Marshall reaches forward just in time, pulling an oxygen mask from my face. I see a mass of dark crud spill on to the pavement rushing below me.

"Can you breathe?" The paramedic asks.

I nod.

"Can you speak?"

"Yes," I say.

The paramedic turns to the US Marshall. "Does she sound hoarse?"

"No," he says, "Not really."

"Good."

"Ma'am," says the Paramedic, "The Harlem Hospital is only a few blocks from here. We're going to get you there now."

We hit something and then the gurney slides forward. Now, I'm in an ambulance. There are two paramedics here, including the one from before. One of the US Marshalls climbs in a moment later.

"What's your name?" I ask.

"US Marshall Johnson," he says, "Sorry I couldn't get you sooner. I couldn't get through the damned door."

I nod at him. Johnson. I'll remember Johnson. He's one of the good guys. I know that now.

The ambulance starts moving. "We've given you morphine," says the paramedic, "The pain won't go away, but it ought to get fuzzy."

I nod. Vomiting helped. I'm feeling clearer headed.

"Do I need to go the hospital?" I ask.

The Paramedic just looks at me.

"Do I need to go the hospital?" I ask again.

"You were just in a major fire, ma'am?"

"Yes, but do I need to go the hospital?"

"You're breathing okay. You have burns, but they look like 2nd degree burns on your hands and knees. You can treat them with antibiotic ointments. You're might also need a bucketload of antibiotics and painkillers."

"And?"

"You should see a doctor."

I see the US Marshall think for a moment. Then he decides something. "Stop the ambulance," he calls out to the driver.

"What?" asks the paramedic.

"Stop the ambulance," says the Marshall.

"Why?" says the paramedic.

"This woman is an FBI Special Agent. I'm guarding her because of a credible threat against her person. While I was sitting outside her apartment door, there was a *fire*. She believes, and *I* believe, she may have been the target of that fire. I don't want her in a public place if she doesn't need to be."

The Paramedic just looks at the two of us.

"Stop the DAMNED VAN!" shouts Marshall Johnson.

I feel a jolt as the driver hits the brakes.

A moment later, Marshall Johnson has the back doors open. I feel the rush of fresh air. I inhale. It burns, but it feels so much better than the air in the apartment had.

"Can you sit up?" Johnson asks.

"I really recommend against it," says the Paramedic.

"I know what I'm doing," answers Johnson.

"But we're almost there!" comes a voice from the front of the ambulance.

I begin to sit up. I'm still dizzy. I feel nauseous. But I'm far better than before. Marshall Johnson takes my hand as I gingerly lower my foot to the floor of the ambulance. Still holding my hand, he jumps down to the ground. I see the armored SUV is stopped right behind us. We're parked right in front of the hospital. The lights of the ambulance are flashing over everything.

I lean forward. I feel suddenly overwhelmed by dizziness. I topple forward. Johnson catches me easily. He tosses me over his shoulder.

"Can you trust the other guy?" I ask, feeling helpless.

"Yeah," says Johnson, "You can trust him."

As we walk away, I hear the paramedic call after us, "Keep her awake! Get somebody in to see her as soon as you can! Get those burns treated!"

"We got it!" says the Marshall.

I'm curious why he's so confident.

My stomach is in knots. I hear the 'other guy' jump down from his seat and open the back for me. Johnson lays me carefully into my seat and belts me in. The other guy hops back in the front. Johnson doesn't. He opens the back of the SUV, grabs something and then slides in next to me.

I look over and see a massive Khaki Green bag with a large red cross on it.

"What's that?"

"Combat First Aid," he says, "I was a medic in Afghanistan."

The other guy turns back to us and asks, "Where to?"

I mumble, exhausted, "Javits."

"You heard the lady," says Johnson. As he opens his kit and begins to pull out ointments and gauze, the other guy floors it and we take off down Lenox Avenue.

I want to feel safe, surrounded by armor and men willing to risk themselves to protect me.

But I don't feel safe.

Even as Johnson gently wraps my burns, my mind frantically searches for the source of the next attack.

I am almost overwhelmed by fear.

Arson

Monday – 8:00 AM

The knocking that wakes me up is incredibly gentle. At that light prompting, I open my eyes and see light streaming through the office blinds. I'm laying on a cot taken from the holding area. My hands and knees are killing me.

I feel like crap.

I roll off the cot, stumble upwards and head for the door. I'd locked from the inside.

"Who's there?" I ask, my voice almost a mumble.

"US Marshall Johnson," comes the reply. "It's eight o'clock ma'am."

Eight? As we drove down to the Javitz Federal Building, SAC Miller arranged for some unfortunate doctor to get summoned to the office in the middle of the night. He checked me out and 15 minutes after getting to the building, I was passed out cold in an empty office (with the good Doctor's blessing). I asked to sleep until 8. I've got to get up. I've got to fight back.

Right now, though, I don't feel like I can manage it.

I unlock and open the door. US Marshall Johnson is there. His hands are also bandaged – although not as extensively as mine. There's a smile on his face. I notice he also has a coffee in a thick paper cup and a large paper bag in his hand.

"For me?" I ask, looking at the coffee.

"Yes," says Johnson, "I figured you'd need it."

He extends the coffee and the bag. I look at them. My hands are bandaged and in incredible pain. I don't think I can pick up the bags.

He notices and pulls them back. He says, "I'll set it up for you in the conference room."

I follow behind him. I am disheveled. There's smoke in my hair, my clothes are charred. As I walk the short distance to the conference room, everybody's eyes are tracking me. This is the FBI; everybody is already at work and everybody already knows what happened to me.

Johnson turns his head as we walk, "If you'd like, I can take a sip of your coffee and a bite of one of the bagels. You know, to make sure they aren't poisoned."

I smile at that. "What kind of bagels did you get?"

"All of them," he says, "I wasn't sure which you'd like."

There's something in his voice that brings me to a stop. Johnson turns back to me.

"Do you flirt with all your protectees?" I ask.

A blush comes to his face. In that moment, I see him in a new light. He's almost six foot tall, he's strong and confident and toned. He's calm under pressure, he's dedicated to his responsibilities. And he's already saved my life once. A woman could do worse.

"No, ma'am," he answers, with the hint of a smile.

"Good," I say, feeling a little special despite myself.

We keep walking. A moment later, he opens the conference room door and I shuffle in. My team is here. I take a seat at the table, remembering that somebody in this group is probably working for Aji.

Johnson puts the coffee in front of me.

"It's iced," he says. That's thoughtful, I tell myself. After all, I had burned my throat the night before. Johnson steps back and I look up at the group gathered around me.

"Where are we?" I ask.

Jason Peters is the Special Agent who has been spearheading our coordination with other agencies. Although fit, he's a slight man who projects an air of friendliness and conciliation. He can turn tough, but his default attitude tends to open doors.

"Immediately after the fire, I spoke with the New York Fire Department. The fire started in the apartment directly below yours. There were noodles on a pot in the kitchen. They were left on too long. The NYFD said it was likely an accident but given the circumstances, we arrested the woman. Her name is Sarah Brown and she's in holding down the hall."

"Has anybody looked into her background?" I ask.

"Yes," says Clara, "We got a warrant and searched her apartment, phone records, public social media posts and Metrocard records. Her apartment was far less damaged than yours. The fire went up. She also left the apartment sooner. She wasn't injured. She didn't get any unusual messages yesterday; her routine was normal for a Sunday. She's a janitor at a hospital. She's commented several times on Aji. Her comments have always been negative. She's suggested that the people he brings on stage are pre-selected and that Aji does it because he loves the attention. Aside from the circumstances, nothing seems amiss at this time."

"Did you run a Ghost Report?" I ask Matthew Crass. The Ghost Report is a phone tracing system that tracks whether a particular phone has had a burner phone near it for extended periods of time. We use it to associate devices, and thus burner phones and their actual owners. We need a warrant to use the system as even users of burner phones have a right to privacy.

"Yes," says Matthew, "The woman doesn't have a burner so nobody called her on one."

"She wouldn't really need to," I say. "Aji probably knew *I* was going to arrest him. After I did, the woman could have received a pre-arranged signal, like somebody waving at her from across the street."

Bill Riley, an expert on complex conspiracies like organized crime or terrorist syndicates, jumps in, "It's possible, but it will be very hard to find evidence of it. And we need evidence to keep holding her."

I nod and gingerly pick up my iced coffee in bandaged hands. The cold liquid provides a mix of pain and relief as it rolls down my tender throat.

"Okay," I say, "I hate to do this, but there's strong evidence Aji knew I was coming yesterday. That suggests somebody in *this* office is giving his group information. It is probably somebody outside this particular group. Because of this, I want you holding information close. Don't share it. Even in the office. Just in case it is one of you, I want you looking over each other's shoulders. You're looking for two things: the passing of information and the failure to do a complete and thorough job. Matthew and Jason, I want the two of you checking each other's work. Clara and Bill, the same for you. To be sure, we'll rotate the reviews each day. I want this to start retroactively, so please share your notes from this morning with each other."

I look at them, hoping I haven't insulted them. Nobody seems offended. They seem to understand why I'm suspicious of even them. I won't catch Aji's team with this kind of supervision, but at least I'm less likely to have my own people undermine me.

I continue, "Okay. Sarah Brown seems like almost every other Aji related case. We have a suspicious situation and no way to tie it to Aji or his team. I assume we haven't seen any special movement from Aji's people, right?"

"Nothing," says Jason, "No calls, no unusual visitors after the arrest. They went back to their hotel and that was it. Radio silence until this morning and even now nothing out of the ordinary is going on."

"If we don't get something connecting them to Sarah Brown, we're going to have to release her," says Clara.

"Has anybody interrogated her?" I ask.

"We talked to her a bit. We didn't get anywhere. She's probably asleep now."

"Okay," I say, "I'll go talk to her. Maybe seeing her victim will get her to open up."

Five minutes later, I open the door to the interrogation room. Sarah Brown is a short and compact black woman. She's slumped over the table in the interrogation room. She isn't handcuffed. Instead, her arms are wrapped beneath her head, providing an ad-hoc pillow. The lights are on their standard brightness setting: bright and very uncomfortable.

We probably should have moved her to holding. She could have lain down there. Nonetheless, a little discomfort can help prod some witnesses. Plus, we know we can get away with holding her in the interrogation room for a few hours.

As I walk into the room, the woman lifts her head from the table. Her skin is the color of milk chocolate. Her eyes are red and puffy with exhaustion. As she sees me, she says, "I told them I want a lawyer."

"We've called a public defender," I say. "He'll be here in a few minutes. In the meantime, you don't have to answer any questions or say anything. Understand?"

The woman nods.

I sit across from her. I've got to get her to talk voluntarily.

I begin to unwrap the loose bandages on my right hand. "You were arrested last night on suspicion of attempted murder. I was the woman you tried to murder."

As I pull the layers of tape off, the lower layers, covered in puss and ointment, are revealed. The pain is shocking, but I keep going.

The woman is trying to look me in the face. But she can't stop herself from stealing glances at my hands. There's a sense of panic in her eyes. I keep unwrapping.

"You almost succeeded. I was moments away from being trapped and dying."

The first raw skin is revealed. Even I can barely look at it. It is red and raw; patches are actually charred.

The woman is horrified. "I'm so sorry," she says, "I just put the noodles on the pot, and I fell asleep by accident. I didn't think I was that tired, but I guess I was. I didn't want to hurt anybody."

I keep unwrapping.

"Ms. Brown, do you know how I became an FBI agent?"

"No, why would I know that?"

"I was a campus police officer at the University of Northern California in Eureka. The FBI recruited me. Do you know how unusual it is for a campus police officer to make the jump to the FBI?"

"No," she says. She looks worried and scared.

"One day I heard a rumor about a video for sale online. It showed the violent rape of a woman. One of our students. I heard about it and then I went and found it. It was easy to get. I just went online and looked for UNC rape video and there it was. I bought that video. I watched part of it. Enough to identify the woman being attacked. She

45

was in fact a student. She led an anarchist group. She had a reputation as an extremely tough person."

I start unwrapping my other hand, the burnt tips of one hand pulling at the bandages at the other.

"I brought her in. To talk to her, privately. I asked her who raped her. She wouldn't say anything. I asked who she was protecting. Nothing. I asked why she – who had spoken up many times about pushing back on the patriarchy – would allow her rapist to walk free. I wanted to help her confront her own horror. But she said nothing. Then she smiled. I remember it so clearly.

"I have a degree in Art History. I'd spent an extraordinary amount of time analyzing and the discussing the faces of men and women in art. I'd spent so much time figuring out why the *Girl with the Pearl Earring* has her lips as she does. Or why the Apostles in the Da Vinci's *Last Supper* each have the facial and body language they do. When I saw that woman smile, I knew something else was happening."

Sarah Brown is watching my hands, her focus is not on my words. She looks up at me, unable to ask "What?" but I can see it in her expression.

"I let the woman go. And then I spent the next week tracing the activities of her group. When they travelled, they rented cars and hotel rooms. They purchased body armor for protests and riots. They bought military-grade clothing and gear for their operations. They were very well funded. I followed the money and realized that she was the one who ran the website I'd bought the video on."

Sarah Brown looks confused.

"I asked her about it later. I just stopped her on one of the campus walks and told her what I'd found. She smiled again. Same smile. She was triumphant. She said she was using the violent rape culture of the patriarchy against it. Men who fantasized about violence against women would pay to see her supposedly being attacked, and she would use their money to overthrow them. There was no crime. When the FBI came to investigate her, I shared what I knew. They were impressed and encouraged me to apply for a job."

46

Sarah Brown knows she shouldn't talk, but she does. "What does that have to do with me?"

"Ms. Brown," I say, "It is a felony to lie to a Federal Agent. If you lie to me, I will work it out and you will go to prison."

She looks at me, her eyes full of fear.

"Ms. Brown, were you instructed to set that fire?"

"No," she says, her composure failing her completely. She starts crying, huge wracking sobs. "I didn't want to start a fire. I just fell asleep. I'm so so sorry you're hurt. Please, please, please believe me. I'm not lying."

I've gotten nowhere. I *know* she has to be involved, but I've got nothing to work with. Her conviction is so convincing that I'm even beginning to doubt myself.

I hate these damned fanatics.

Just then the door opens and the lawyer, a public defender I know, steps in.

"What are you doing to my client," she asks, her voice brusque. Part of it is just to show Sarah she's standing up for her. She won't really push things too far. While she'll deal with Sarah Brown for a day or two, she'll be dealing with us for the rest of her career.

I stand up, gingerly gathering my bandages back together.

"We were just talking," I say, "Now, she's free to go."

Sarah's eyes track my every step as I walk out of the room.

Angle

Monday – 9:30 AM

Over the past year, I've conducted dozens of interviews just like Sarah Brown's. True believers who won't confess anything about what they've done and why.

Somewhere in the background, I hear Clara, "We can get a subpoena and look into her private social media messages." Then Jason, "We can look into when she rented the apartment. Maybe she moved in after you, which would be a red flag." Matthew, "We can check CCTV to see if she'd acted unusually on her way home from work."

I ignore them all. My hands are a ball of pain. Johnson is gently cleaning them with a wet cloth, wiping away old ointment with a striking tenderness. As I'd come out of the interrogation room, Johnson had told me not to pull that trick again. The gauze I have is designed to remain in place until the burn has healed. I truly appreciate his concern.

I'm not ignoring my team because of the pain of my hands, or the pleasure of Johnson's care. I'm ignoring them because everything they suggest is hopeless. I look up and say, "None of these ideas have ever worked before and they aren't going to work now. Aji's team is just too good at covering their tracks."

The group looks defeated.

Clara says, "But we have to try. It's what we do."

"We don't have to be pig-headed about it," I say, "We need to be smart. We need to be targeted. Doing what we've done before has a tiny chance of yielding something useful. We'll do it. All of it, if we need to. But things have changed."

"How?" asks Jason Peters, the interagency coordinator.

"*We've arrested Aji.* We have what we need to charge him."

Bill Riley, the conspiracy expert, says, "That isn't enough. We need to wrap up the whole group. You've said it yourself."

48

I want to hold up my hands, to shush them. But I can't. "Everybody," I say, "I want to get them all. They just tried to kill me, an FBI agent. I can't let that go unanswered and neither can you."

"Okay," says Bill, "So what do you want to do?"

"Let's go back to the basics. Motive, means, and opportunity. Maybe our current situation can open something new up."

"We still don't know the motive," says Jason.

"Yes, we do," says Clara, "These people want money and power."

"They aren't making much money," says Bill, "They raise a fair amount but whatever they don't spend on cheap hotels, fuel for their bus and inexpensive events is given to charity. There's no war chest being assembled."

"That we can see," says Clara.

"We've dug into this," says Matthew, "We've tracked committed donors to see if they've been giving money off the books. They haven't. It isn't money."

Clara says, "*We* may not think it's money. But you have to consider where they came from."

I say, "No matter where they came from, if they were doing it for money, they'd be keeping some of it."

Clara grimaces. She doesn't agree, but we've been through this argument a million times.

"Does what's happened since Aji's arrest tell us anything about motive?" I ask.

Clara says, "Well, you thought it was about reputation. But when you offered to keep things quiet, in return for giving up his team, he didn't bite."

"Okay, so maybe reputation isn't the point," I say.

"Or maybe he figures it's shot anyways," says Jason.

"Or... maybe he thinks he can outplay us in the media and his reputation will be fine," says Clara.

"Maybe. Aside from reputation and money, we've got power and influence. Anything else come to mind?"

Johnson looks up from treating my hands. He's applying ointment to both of them. They hurt like hell, but even the first daubs of ointment are relieving the pain. The gauze is waiting on the table.

"He could *really* believe it," Johnson says.

"How could he possibly believe it?" I ask, "That's absurd."

Johnson answers, "His people could be the ones behind it. They could have set him up and convinced him he's got some mystical ability while *they* run everything in the background."

"So, he actually *thinks* he's a holy man?" asks Clara.

"A mafia don who doesn't know it," says Bill with a whistle.

"What a con that would be," says Jason.

"But why?" asks Matthew, the computer analyst. "Why would they do it, and why would they choose Aji? And I know we're not talking means and opportunity yet, but how would they pull it off?"

"One question at a time. Let's start with why they'd choose Aji."

"That's easy, he was convenient," says Bill, the conspiracy guy.

"How?"

"Well, he grew up in California. He was born Michael Abakar. His parents died in a car crash and he escaped the foster system when he was 12. He'd been on the run for 6 years. I imagine he wanted family more than anything. His parents had immigrated from the Garubia. These new immigrants come along. He runs into them in South Carolina and he gloms on to them. He even changes his name to Aji to fit in. They're like extended family. He's an easy mark."

It's a solid theory, and a new one. Nobody says anything.

"Why would they do it?" I ask as Johnson finishes with the ointment and begins to loosely wrap fresh gauze around my right hand.

I'm met with blank stares.

"Let's go over their history. Maybe with this new theory something will pop out." I say.

"Okay," says Clara. "Here's what we know. There are 15 of them. They applied, together, for special refugee status at the US Embassy in Duomba. They were all former child soldiers in the Chosen People's Liberation Force, a brutal group led by Mombato Yogula. Yogula had died, maybe been killed and his army had broken up. These kids ended up in Duomba, but they were having a very hard time of it. For all the nice things the locals said, they hated child soldiers – especially those from the CPLF. They were harassed and beaten. So, they applied for, and received, refugee status. The US admitted them. Although they were sent to different US cities, they quickly reunited. Almost immediately, they joined up with Aji."

"They could be looking for family too," says Jason. "The whole ruse could be about creating what they had, a family. But it's twisted, because they were child soldiers for a religious whack job. For them, a family is about violence, intimidation, group loyalty and following some charismatic religious crazy. They chose Aji because he was convenient and didn't have all their baggage. He was American enough to be accepted."

It's a dark picture, but perhaps a plausible one.

Bill chimes in, "They don't mind killing people. They're used to it. They're just carrying on the legacy of Mombato Yogula," says Bill.

"What if they lied on their immigration application?" says Jason.

"Why?"

"Think about it," says Jason, "They were African child soldiers. They know how to shoot people with AK-47s and machete them if they're out of bullets. Carefully covering their footsteps while running a massive conspiracy in the United States would not fall within their skill set. How'd they get good enough to hide what they're doing from us?"

"Holy cow," says Bill Riley, whistling loudly.

We all know what he's talking about. Duomba is a center of any number of failed state issues. Yes, there are recently disbanded groups of child soldiers. Yes, there is the occasional military coup. But there is also a flourishing Islamic insurgency. Both the Islamic State and Al Qaeda are active in the area.

"They're terrorists?" asks Jason.

"Maybe," I say, "But what does Aji give them? Why go to all the trouble?"

"Travel," every voice says simultaneously.

Bill spells it out, "They can go everywhere in the country, they can assemble terrorist networks, they can fundraise. It's the perfect cover. They can hide in plain sight. All they need to do is arrange a few miracles and a few curses and they have a free pass."

"That's a hell of a conspiracy," I say, "But they don't have a free pass. We're trying very hard to find out what they're up to. So, what are they gaining? I can't imagine they'd be any less able to travel, fundraise and organize without Aji as a front man."

"I guess nothing," says Bill.

"Maybe a combination is true. Maybe they were some kind of specialists trained by Yogula. Maybe he's carrying on some sort of crazy plan from beyond the grave."

"You should write fantasy novels," says Matthew. His face is deadly serious. "That's some good stuff."

A chuckle goes around the room.

"Wait a moment," says Clara, a smile spreading across her face. "Bill's theory doesn't have to make complete sense to be useful?"

"How?" I ask.

"Why don't we use the Islamic terrorism story to trigger their network. And then we can see what happens and see how they communicate."

All the around the table, heads nod in appreciation of the idea.

Deception

Monday – 3:00 PM

It is five hours later, and I'm being driven back to Brooklyn. This time the destination isn't Prospect Park, but "The Worst Hotel in Brooklyn." The neighborhood around the hotel is populated by a mix of low-slung and run-down looking apartment buildings and even more depressed-looking stucco townhouses. The place is both too far from Manhattan to be desirable, and too close to be attractive. The whole area is dominated by the Belt Parkway, a rumbling freeway that passes several stories above the ground. Every day, commuters pass over this neighborhood, reading billboards at the tops of buildings. They never see what lays beneath. It is the kind of place defined by laundromats, self-storage units and, yes, motels. The motels cater to NYU Langone Hospital or out-of-town visitors on low budgets. Given their customer base, rooms are cheap, and appearances are largely unimportant.

Aji's hotel, the one his group and their followers have overrun, is a five-story affair with 68 rooms. They've taken up the top two floors, 24 rooms in all. We've read the online reviews, trying to get a picture of the place. Poor room service, deceptive management. Low prices. Of course, we doubted anything was lacking in the service provided to Aji and his people. People seemed to really believed that if you did right by Aji, the universe would do right by you.

We hadn't just looked at the rooms online, of course. In the five hours since our conversation in the conference room we'd pulled schematics from City Records. We'd set up cameras with telescopic lenses facing every window in the place, watching for signs and signals. We'd even parked a special FBI van, loaded with systems derived US Air Force surveillance systems, to watch for non-standard radio, IR or other broadcasts from the small building. Because we didn't know what was going on, we wanted to be ready for anything.

Only then did I call Aji's second in command, a man named Der'nube. He had only one name – I guess it was rare enough that

that didn't matter. I told him I needed to meet with him, to interview him after the attack I'd suffered the night before. It wasn't the first time I'd met him – we'd interviewed him time and again, looking for connections to the murders and mysterious injuries. The team wanted me to go in heavy, but I decided against it. Aji's people specialized in the unclear and the hidden. Nothing was going to be unclear in this case. I was walking into their world, not in a park full of partisans but a hotel with booked rooms and known IDs. FBI agents would be posted in the lobby and outside. It would be clear who was responsible if anything happened to me so I could assume nothing would happen to me. Johnson would stay with me the entire time.

As I enter the lobby, every eye seems to pass over me suspiciously. I'm not wearing an FBI vest, but Johnson is clearly armed and serving some protective role. The place is full. There's a noxious smell wafting in from what is normally a breakfast room. I assume it is wet fufu, a nasty smelling food from Central Africa. I can feel the thrum of the nearby freeway radiating through the concrete of the building.

I see a tall black man in his early 20s standing near the elevator. He gestures for me to follow him. Wordlessly, the three of us enter the elevator. He punches the button for the top floor. Shortly after, we enter a poorly lit hall and are guided to Room 506.

The door is opened by another tall African man, Der'nube himself.

"Hello again, Neisha," he says with a grimace. His accent is thick.

I just nod. He notices my hands. I see his face shift slightly from anger, to genuine concern. It is like a shadow of Aji's face; care in the service of menace.

"I'm sorry about your hands," he says softly, "I guess that's why you're here."

"Yes, I need to ask you some questions."

He stands inside and gestures me into the room. We're the only people there. I notice, alongside the small TV, old chair and beat up mattress that there is a small trunk covered in an unusually patterned cloth. I've seen it before, on previous visits. I wonder if something inside the trunk is core to their communications. Nothing else in the room holds the least bit of mystery.

By the time I sit on the edge of the bed, he's gotten over his concern. "So, you have more questions? You intimidate, harass and badger a man of G-d and those who stand with him. It continues day and night. You watch our events, follow our people and bug our phones. All because of some looney conspiracy. Now you've arrested Aji himself. And now you just have some questions? I'll talk to you, but I'm not happy to do it."

"That's okay," I say, "Officially I'm here to ask you about your connections to Sarah Brown. But you'll deny everything. I really came here to gloat."

Der'nube doesn't say anything.

"I've got Aji in a cell. We're arraigning him at midnight tonight. We've got his case locked up tight. I was worried I wouldn't be able to get rid of you guys when I got a phone call this morning."

"Who from?" he asks.

"A friend at Immigration and Customs Enforcement. It turns out they believe you've lied on your immigration application?"

"Lied? They have a box asking if you've been part of a terrorist organization. I checked 'yes'. They asked if I've been arrested? Yes again. Trafficked in any controlled substance, been a member of a totalitarian party, engaged in genocide, tortured, injured, raped. 'yes', 'yes', 'yes', 'yes' and 'yes.' We were all kids in a vicious militia. We did terrible things. I admitted it all. What could I possibly have wanted to lie about?"

I smile.

"What?" he asks.

"You could have lied about *which* militia. And you could have lied about whether you left."

The accusation hangs in the air. His face turns ashen. He knows what I'm implying.

"They might not just deport you," I say, "They might send you to Guantanamo, or worse. I'm done with this case. They'll handle you from here on out."

I get up from the bed and walk to the door.

"It's been a pleasure knowing you, Der'nube. I'll show myself out."

With Johnson following me, I make my way down the hall, to the elevator and out of the lobby. A large black SUV picks me up outside the front door. I sit in the back and pop on a headset to listen to the live feed produced by the many eyes watching the motel.

I expect to wait before Der'nube makes his move. He doesn't. We haven't even reached the corner when a voice comes online. "He's picked up his phone."

I listen to the live description of the man's actions.

"He's looking up a number on his phone. It is the number for an Adam Killingsworth."

Another voice comes on, "I'm cross-referencing now. Mr. Killingsworth is an officer at Immigration and Customs Enforcement."

There's a ringing noise. "Playing the call now," says the first voice.

"Adam here," comes a business-like voice.

"Adam, this is Der'nube."

"Oh, hi," says Adam, cheerfully.

"Listen, I've heard a rumor that you guys are going to come and deport us. Is it true?"

I hear a clicking of keys. Adam seems to be checking something. After a minute, he says, "Der'nube, I haven't heard anything. Of course, you understand that even if I had, I couldn't tell you. Right?"

"Right," says Der'nube. A pause. "Thanks for the help."

"No help, no problem," says Adam.

A moment later, they hang up.

Over the next three hours, Der'nube circulates through the rooms of his compatriots. But they make no suspicious calls. They wave no flags from the windows and they emit no unusual electronic bursts. We tail those who leave the hotel, but they engage in no suspicious meetings. There is nothing but a phone call that we traced, easily.

We've accomplished exactly nothing.

It is time to shoot the hostage.

Riot

Wednesday –8:00 AM

As I step into the interrogation room, Aji looks up at me with that same enticing smile. He seems almost completely unaffected by his days in holding.

I haven't been imprisoned. Nonetheless, I am a physical wreck.

We'd held the 'shoot the hostage' press conference the day before. We made a big deal out of everything. There was a purpose to it. It was simple: we'd reach out to the public and they'd tell us what we needed to know. They'd give us the evidence of coercion, racketeering and organized intimidation that must fuel Aji's organization.

The presser had been staged in Foley Square, almost adjacent to the Federal Building. We were on the steps of the massive monument there: *The Triumph of the Human Spirit*. It's a 300-ton black granite sculpture celebrating the perseverance of Africans through the trials of slavery. I remember standing in front of that monument and looking at the gathering crowd. To my left was the Federal Building and to my right the New York Supreme Court. I put them all together in my mind and realized that I was standing at the nexus of government, justice and humanity.

It was a good place to be.

Even as we waited for the 11 o'clock start of the conference, things were tense. Yes, reporters had assembled – dozens of them. They were not alone though. Thousands of Aji supporters had shown up, crowding the space between Lafayette and Center streets. There were also a few hundred anti-Aji activists. The two groups formed like-minded clumps. When they drew close, I could see the friction between them. Shouting, gesticulating. Argument. Nobody was fighting, but it seemed like it could turn violent at the drop of a hat.

I asked SAC Miller if we should take the conference inside the Federal Building. He said no. We couldn't let the protestors, especially ones from a movement as influential as Aji's, see themselves pushing the Federal Government around. We were going to stay, and by staying we'd be making a statement about the power and position of law and order.

We weren't just going to stand there though. We were going to demonstrate that power. SAC Miller made a few calls and a few minutes later, ranks of riot police were already beginning to assemble the edge of the square. A line of them formed behind the reporters – keeping the press conference separate from the mob. Finally, an FBI armored truck pulled up behind us – giving us a quick getaway in case things got ugly. That was our only sign of weakness.

I'd come to the square reflecting on how different my second appearance on national media would be. The first time, Aji had been in control. The first time, he'd been toying with me. This time, *we'd* be the ones conducting events.

Now, though, I wasn't so sure. Between the riot police, the truck and US Marshall Johnson, I knew I'd be safe. But I didn't feel like I was in control.

By the time 11 o'clock came, the press was beginning to get a bit nervous. The crowd behind them was getting louder and more animated. The whole square was crackling with an ugly energy. Normally we would have waited a few minutes to build up tension for the press conference itself, but not today. So, only a few seconds after 11, SAC Miller stepped up to microphone. Despite the tension in the air, Miller's demeaner was confident, capable and completely self-assured. The press, largely sandwiched between us and the crowd, calmed noticeably.

Then he began to speak. "Good afternoon – "

Then, as if on cue, the massive crowd launched into a loud chat "Free Aji! Free Aji! Free Aji!"

Miller *seemed* unaffected. He kept reading. But even I couldn't hear him clearly. The speakers were being drowned out by the crowd. We were there to tell people what the kind of person Aji actually was – but despite the police presence, it seemed like the crowd might just stop us from doing so. A few inaudible sentences in and Miller stopped. He looked around, just a little desperate.

"FREE AJI! FREE AJI! FREE AJI!"

The crowd, sensing victory, had gotten louder.

It was Johnson who came up with the answer. He held up his phone and nodded at it. SAC Miller got the hint. He called over one of the technicians. They had a quick, barely audible conversation. A few phone calls followed. Then the technician began to reroute the cabling. Instead of going to the speaker system, it was routed into the SAC's phone.

A few minutes later, somebody came dashing out of the FBI building with a stack of papers. They made their way to the steps and then began handing the papers out. They were directions to an online meeting.

It was a weird set up. We spoke into the microphone and our words were broadcast onto the online meeting. The reporters, standing right in front of us, could then listen in on their phones. It wasn't a perfect solution, but it wasn't surrender.

Ten minutes after 11, we were able to start again.

The whole crowd of reporters, and the people on the stage, were holding their phones to their ears. Then the SAC began to speak again. I hadn't called into the conference. I didn't hear a word he said. I knew the gist though, he was just setting the stage and introducing me.

He gestured towards me, and I stepped forward, surrounded by the chants. I leaned towards the microphone and began to read my prepared statement. I spoke slowly and loudly. "Good morning, I am Special Agent Neisha Jackson. I head a task force that was assembled just over a year ago to investigate a pattern of deaths and injuries related to critics of Mr. Aji Abakar. We looked into a number of incidents but we were unable to connect them directly to Mr. Abakar.

"However, two weeks ago, we managed to connect Mr. Abakar to the death of John Buckner using witness testimony as well as fingerprint and DNA evidence. We received an arrest warrant and executed it late Sunday night.

"While Mr. Abakar will be charged in this case, we believe he and his associates have been involved in many other physical attacks against his critics. We believe he is operating a complex racketeering operation using the public conceit that those who bless him are blessed and those who curse him are cursed. In fact, we believe, he arranges favors for those who support him and directly arranges the injury or death against those who oppose him. For this reason, we are asking members of the public to come forward.

"If you have information that could uncover the means by which either benefit or harm are arranged, we need your help. It is our belief that the incarceration of Mr. Abakar's confederates is critical for public safety.

"For this reason, the FBI is offering up to one million dollars for information that leads to the arrests and convictions of his confederates.

"If you have any information, please call us at 1-800-CALLFBI. Thank you."

I looked up to see the reporters pulling their phones from their ears and frantically typing questions into them. I looked at the SAC's phone. Dozens of questions are cueing up.

"Answer whatever you'd like," said the SAC in an almost shout.

I nodded and picked one question from the list: "Can you provide more details about how you connected Mr. Abakar to the murder?"

I stepped back up to the microphone. The assembled press, still almost overwhelmed by the chants, lifted their phones back to their ears. "Somebody asked if we could provide more details on the connection between Mr. Abakar and the murder. I can. We had assembled a list of possible targets due to online content produced by those targets. Mr. Buckner was on that list. When there was a gas leak and explosion at his house it triggered automatic follow up. We investigated as part of our task force's regular operations. We discovered the man who had caused the leak, a transient named Mr. Elvis Brown. We worked backward from Mr. Brown to Mr. Abakar."

My answer had been rehearsed. I shared only the outlines of the story. I didn't mention that although the killer successfully hid his face from CCTV cameras near the house, we still managed to follow him until he was no longer so careful. I didn't mention the interrogation and his claim that Mr. Abakar had sent him. I didn't mention Elvis' attempt to escape murder charges by claiming Abakar had only asked him to cut the gas line, not trigger the explosion. Finally, I didn't mention that CCTV and Metro Card records showed Mr. Abakar in Hunts Point earlier that same evening, with ample opportunity to meet with Elvis Brown in a blind spot outside a bar called the Railroad Lounge.

All of those details will come out in court.

I looked back at the phone.

This time the SAC was looking over my shoulder. He stepped up to the microphone. "Somebody asked why we didn't protect the possible targets – instead of waiting for them to be attacked. The answer is that there were simply too many to protect. We had over a thousand names and we had no way of knowing which were under imminent threat or how they might be struck. However, FBI teams did visit each of the targets we identified to inform them of the possible danger and review their personal security. John Buckner was visited just two days before his death."

Back to the phone and then another answer, "The FBI uses a sophisticated statistical analysis tool to determine the likelihood of coincidence in a pattern of attacks. Despite there being thousands of possible targets, the likelihood of these attacks being coincidence has been determined to be very low."

I saw a question I hadn't expected: "Was Special Agent Jackson picked as head of the task force because the FBI didn't want a white man or woman arresting a prominent young black leader?"

The question stuck with me. Was *that* why I was selected? Was it all about optics? I thought about answering, but the SAC scrolls right past it. Another question, a predictable one: "Is Special Agent Jackson afraid of the curse?"

I stepped up to the microphone for this one. The phones go back to the ears. "One of you has asked if I'm afraid of the curse. There is no curse. What there is an organization dedicated to harming critics of Mr. Aji."

I held up my hands.

"There has already been one attempt on my life since the arrest was made. It is possible there will be more. I am under protection from the US Marshall's service. Nonetheless, when dealing with a sophisticated and violent criminal enterprise, risk is unavoidable. Our desire to rapidly bring this group to justice is partially driven by the danger they pose so long as they remain free."

Another volley of questions followed but SAC Miller held up his hands and declared that that would be it for now. That didn't slow the crowd though. Sensing our departure, the chanting got even louder. Then the crowd began to advance towards the stage. They weren't throwing rocks or Molotov cocktails. They were simply moving forward, pushing against the line of riot shields.

The riot police tried to hold their line, but the mass of people was too great. They were being pushed slowly backwards. The reporters scrambled towards us in a near panic. It was then that *we* retreated. SAC Miller, Marshall Johnson, myself and the technicians all made a dash for the armored truck.

We scrambled in the back as the noise outside grew ever louder. Johnson closed the doors – dampening the chanting just a touch – and the truck began to roll forward. It didn't have far to go. We'd just turn right on Reed Street, drive two blocks to Church, make two quick rights and pull into the underground parking lot at the Federal Building. It would take five minutes, tops.

We sat in the bench seats, safe and secure. I was on the right of the truck. The others were seated opposite me. There was plenty of space.

We made the turn on Reade. Quickly, the sound of the crowd was erased by the buildings between us. We stopped at Broadway. I assume the light was red. Nobody was following us.

Then the truck moved forward.

A moment later everything turned sideways.

I was thrown into the air. I knew, instantly, that we'd been attacked. But I knew more than that.

As I flew between one side of the truck and the other, I was struck by a simple insight. We knew Aji's African minders didn't order the attack – we were watching them too carefully. We were watching Aji too. Even with an informant in the FBI it was unlikely *he'd* ordered the attack.

That left one option.

As I drew close to the opposite wall of the truck, I tried to catch myself with my right arm. I saw it snap in front of me.

In that moment, though, I knew there was a hidden agent; somebody we didn't know about was calling the shots.

That was the last thought I had before the rest of my body slammed into the side of the truck.

I passed out, for the second time in three days.

We found out later what had happened. We'd been hit by a delivery truck. The truck's own data systems told us the driver's foot had jammed onto his accelerator. Video footage had confirmed that he'd run into us at close to 50 miles an hour. He'd had a history of epilepsy, but medication had successfully controlled it for years. Online, he'd been a prominent critic of Aji's. We never got the chance to question him though. He'd been killed instantly at the scene.

I'd been in the hospital for the rest of the day. Marshall Johnson had been hovering over me. My team kept me informed though. We never got any credible calls from the public. We learned nothing from the press conference itself. That didn't bother me. I'd learned a lot from that attack itself.

I knew now that I wasn't dealing with Aji and I wasn't dealing with Aji's crew. Somebody else was calling the shots.

There was a hidden agent, and my task was simply to find them.

Standoff

Wednesday – 9:05 AM

The hidden agent is the reason why I'm sitting on a flimsy plastic folding chair in Aji's holding cell. Aji himself is sitting on his small FBI-issued cot. His knees are just a few feet from mine. Despite myself I feel an energy bridging the gap between us. I want to be further from him, but it's hard to get further away in a cell that is only 8 feet by 8 feet.

I pull my eyes away from Aji and watch as Marshall Johnson steps up onto a small stool. In his hand is a wide roll of black electrical tape. Carefully, he begins to apply it to both the lens and the tiny patch of microphone that make up the surveillance system.

I'd wanted to apply the tape myself. But between my hands and my broken arm, it wasn't an option. Also, while I may not want to admit it on the eve of the most important interrogation I'm ever likely to perform, it is, well, pleasant, to watch Marshall Johnson work.

I glance around the room, as the Marshall works, taking in the thick coat of sterile white paint that seems to cover every surface. The smell of that paint, applied months or years before, seems to hang oppressively in the still air. As if the paint weren't enough, harsh white LED lights in protective metal frames shine down from the ceiling. They are accompanied by a patch of intense sunlight poking through a tiny semi-opaque east-facing window. The sunlight is the only evidence of a world outside. Even sound is kept at bay by the thickness of the walls and thickness of the paint.

This is a space completely separate from the world. It is meant to frighten those who occupy it.

Thirty seconds after stepping up onto the stool, Johnson steps down. His handywork, a patchwork of black tape, is like a scar on the surface of the pure white walls.

I turn back to Aji, watching his face, hoping for some sort of relief. I don't see anything. Instead, just as before, he is smiling. His eyes almost seem to be drinking me in. Their calm and their intensity disturb me.

"Thank you, Marshall Johnson," I say, "You can wait outside."

Johnson looks at me, uncertain. Then he steps from the small cell and closes the heavy door behind him.

Aji just watches.

"It's just us, now," I say, stating the obvious.

"Yes," says Aji. I'm hoping for more. But there is nothing more.

"Aji," I say, "We're alone because I realized there's a hidden actor at work in this case. Somebody other than yourself or your lieutenants tried to kill me yesterday."

Aji seems genuinely surprised upset. "I'm sorry to hear that," he says. I might just be on the right track.

"You're a tough young man. You were homeless and on the run for six years. But somebody else is a whole lot scarier. They convinced a delivery truck driver to risk his own life to attack me. I don't know how they did it. I covered the cameras, so you'd feel safe. We're alone and we can work together to go after those who are really responsible for John Buckner's death."

Aji says, "Covering the cameras won't change anything. I hope the truck driver is okay, though."

I don't answer his question. Instead, I glance around the room, theatrically, "Don't you want to breathe free air again?"

There is no answer.

Unbidden, an idea pops into my head. "If you want. I can remove my shirt and slacks and you can verify that I have no kind of wire or recording device."

I don't quite know what I want him to say. His breath catches almost involuntarily. Then, his eyes locked on mine, he says, "That isn't necessary."

"What will it take for you turn on whoever is actually running things?"

Aji doesn't answer, he just continues to smile.

"I have the power of the United States Federal Government behind me. I can bring whoever it is to bear. Just help me out."

Silence.

I try to square the Aji I see with one cowed by some other party. Aji acts like a leader. He sees himself as a leader. He doesn't seem frightened or cowed. Is it all just an act? Or is he doing his best to lead despite the situation he finds himself in?

"I can protect you." I say.

He says nothing. I want him to speak. I want him to reach out to me. I want my theory to be right and I want to protect him. But he says nothing.

I don't know what else to do. I don't know what other plan to implement. I thought this would work. I thought I could separate Aji from his confederate.

But the man isn't budging.

As we sit there, I find my perspective changing. There may well be a hidden agent, but Aji will not turn against him. Aji may not be alone, but he is still a part of the problem. He won't help me. Fear is not the reason why.

I sit there, wondering what I can do to break him open – to unlock the truth. As the minutes pass, the silence becomes its own reality. It seems like a challenge. I have to overcome this man. I can't let him control me. I have to win, no matter else happens.

That's when I realize that I *will* sit there until the man in front of me finally begins to speak. I *will* have that little victory.

As more and more time passes, my mind begins to fill the unnatural emptiness that defines the space. I actually begin to hear the ticking of a clock that isn't there, marking the passage of time that I cannot measure.

Aji says nothing. Our knees almost touching, he just sits on his cot. Watching me. Somehow, he seems fundamentally content.

I know, though, that he's going to speak.

Eventually he will speak.

I imagine the minutes have turned into hours. But I can't tell. All I know is that I'm feeling the first pangs of hunger. Our silence might be broken by circumstance. I can't starve the prisoner; it could invalidate our whole prosecution.

When he asks for food, I have to provide it.

I don't want to provide food, though. His confederates have hurt me. They've burned me and battered me, and I want some bit of retaliation.

I want Aji to starve.

Aji seems to sense it, but he doesn't shift uncomfortably. He doesn't squirm. Instead, the warmth in his eyes, the projected care and concern (and even admiration), seem to dial up – like he has the levels programmed into his interpersonal interface.

He is displaying warmth, but I know he wants me to be afraid; like I was when I first interrogated him. This time I won't bend. I won't flee. So, we sit. In total silence. Alone. Locked in combat.

If nothing else, when he finally asks for food or water, I will have won something.

My hunger grows, but *he* does not speak.

Aji is no monk, sworn to silence. Eventually, he will speak. I know it.

As the day passes, the sun's light weakens in the east-facing window. It is slowly being supplanted by the unnatural glare of the LEDs.

Still, Aji does not move or speak.

Hours must have passed. As the light in the window begins to reveal the first touches of night, I realize I must be running out of time. Whether or not he asks, I have to feed him.

I feel my anger rising, surging, charging up through me. *I will defeat this man. I will destroy this man.* I feel my conviction rising to a crescendo. The ticking of the imaginary clock disappears. The white walls disappear. My sense of time vanishes.

There is just me and him. And I will destroy him.

I find that I want to stand. I want to shout. I want to rise up and strike him, hard. I want to wipe the façade of warmth from his hateful face.

The urge is growing, even though I know giving in would hand Aji yet another victory. The cameras are off. Nobody would know if I hit Aji. I could say he fell. I meant to break him down, but he is breaking me down.

I resist the temptation.

And then I falter.

My muscles tense, readying me for a leap forward. A leap and then a strike with my good arm.

Just before I rise, Aji speaks, "I will never forgive that man. His words of comfort misled me. His words, delivered in hope of gathering followers from among the weak and fearful, killed my brother. I will never forgive him. But vengeance is not my path. Instead, I will show that there is a better road. Rather than building my life on the quicksand of superstition, I will establish it on the firm rock of reason. I will rise above that man. My vengeance will be his shame."

I stare at Aji, shocked at his words. Silenced.

"How did you get that?" I ask.

He ignores me. He says, "I think you got it wrong."

"HOW DID YOU GET THAT?" I demand.

"I have a source." Of course, he has a source.

"That essay is none of your business."

"Neisha, you've opened every record of mine that has interested you. So why can't I do the same?"

I feel like telling him that I'm The Law and that gives me the right. But an argument about The Law won't get me victory or information. But just quoting the essay has given me something. Whoever his informants are, they would have left a trail when they found that essay.

Aji says, again, "I think you got it wrong."

"It was *my* college essay," I say, "about *my* life. You can't say that I got it wrong."

"Is that an argument based on reason or superstition?"

"How the hell did you get it?"

"It was in your file, Neisha. Your FBI background file. I simply read the records that others collected. That's not what's important. What's important is that you got it wrong."

"This is ridiculous," I say, "How can you possibly know me better than I know myself."

"You live in Harlem," he says.

"What? Why does that matter?"

"Why do you live in Harlem?"

I don't really know the reason. "I just do."

"You ran from South Chicago. As far from South Chicago as you could imagine. You were running from the day LaMarcus died. You went from being a middling student to valedictorian of your high school. You went from watching others run to becoming one of the top high-school sprinters in the state of Illinois. You did everything you could to get out of South Chicago."

"I just wanted to succeed."

"No, you didn't *just* want to succeed. You had a compelling life story as well as fantastic grades and superb athleticism. You could have gone to any college in the country. You could have gone to the Ivy League. But you didn't want to go to Yale or Penn or Columbia and live in the midst of broken urban neighborhoods. You even avoided Cornell, perhaps fed up with freezing winters. You chose the University of Northern California, Eureka. You chose *Eureka*, one of the whitest schools in the United States. You chose European Art History. You *chose* a bland northern Californian accent. You were running from *everything* South Chicago represents. So why are you living in Harlem?"

"I don't know why."

"So, maybe I do know you better than you know yourself."

"Okay, Mr. Holy Man, why do *you* think I live in Harlem?"

"I think you live in Harlem because you know, in those hidden parts of your soul, that the pastor was right."

"Right? He promised me blessing and my brother died."

"But he was right."

"Right about what exactly?"

"Neisha, you live in Harlem because you know that all the European Art History in the world couldn't cover up the truth he shared."

"What truth?"

"The truth of his mission. His mission was to raise up his community. You *know*, beyond any reason, how important that mission is. His means was to hold onto whatever human pillars he could, your mother included. And you *know*, beyond any reason, that communities are built on human pillars. *That's* why you live in Harlem. To lift up that community."

Am I really following in the path the pastor set for me?

"You live in Harlem because you're done trying to run from who you really are. The pastor was never really the target of your hatred. You stopped running when you became a cop. And you became a cop because you hate the kind of men who killed your brother. Evil men. They are your true target."

"There, Aji, your information is lacking. I'm only a cop because nobody would take a black woman from South Chicago seriously as a curator of European Art."

"Really? From Art History to police work?"

"*That* was pure coincidence. I was looking for a job. I read an article about Art History and policing. It talked about police going to galleries to learn how to observe and interpret little cues to understand a bigger picture. Things like expressions, brush strokes, lighting or the positioning of limbs. I thought, maybe I could go the other way and be an art historian who became a cop."

He just looks at me, like he's expecting me to take the next step. I say, "Are you about to suggest G-d put the article there to guide me on this path?"

"No," he says, "I'm suggesting that *you* reacted to the article the way you did – by applying for jobs in law enforcement – because, deep down, you already knew you wanted justice. *You* made coincidence into reality. If it hadn't been that article, it would have been something else."

Is he right? Is that why I became a cop?

"You're becoming the pillar that pastor saw."

"I hate that pastor. You know why I hate him." Even as I say it, though, I begin to doubt it.

"You don't hate the pastor. You're following the path he showed you. His path is righteous. Your hatred is for those who are truly evil. The kinds of men who killed your brother."

"I hate the pastor," I say, weakly.

"No," says Aji, "You hate G-d."

I don't know if I even believe there is a G-d. But if there is some force behind what has happened, then I do hate it. G-d, if there is a G-d, should have protected me. He should have protected LaMarcus. We were His servants, and we were betrayed.

There are tears coming to my eyes.

"It's okay," says Aji, quietly, "I hate G-d too."

I look at him, and I feel a sudden wave of kinship. I hate the man, and yet there is kinship.

"Why?" I whisper, "Why do you hate G-d?"

"Neisha, I have seen evil you can hardly imagine. I have seen it flourish. And I have seen G-d stand by and do nothing. What else can I do but hate."

I have no answer. Silence returns to the room. But it is not heavy. In this silence, nothing is muted. The room feels like an exposed nerve, pain hovering right below the surface.

Then Aji speaks again, "I think the greatest people start with hate. Then, somehow, they find trust and love. But *I* don't know how they do it. I don't know how you can see past the pain."

"All I see is pain," I say, "LaMarcus is dead. He died walking home with me. He died because I wasn't careful. If there is a G-d, why would G-d do that? Why would He lead me down that path? Why would He kill that beautiful little boy?"

I don't mean for Aji to answer. I just want to ask. Time and again, in my dreams, LaMarcus has asked me, but I've never asked anybody else.

Aji smiles again. That warm smile. But this time it is bittersweet. "Neisha, I can't understand. I don't think we're meant to. The best I can offer is this: We use the physical, the rational, the reasonable, to build and define our world. We work with the concrete. But G-d exists in another reality. The reality of the spiritual. Where we fashion our physical reality, G-d fashions souls. For Him, bones and blood and pain and joy are simply tools. They are like chisels striking marble to uncover the beauty within."

I let the Aji's words hang there. G-d is fashioning souls, like the soul of LaMarcus. Finally, after a long difficult pause, I say, "LaMarcus *was* beautiful."

"I know," says Aji. Then he whispers, barely audibly, "So are you."

For a second, I think he's talking about me *as a woman*. The idea excites me. Then, a moment later, I understand what he's actually saying. The idea hits me like a slap. He's saying that LaMarcus died to raise *me* up. I want to argue. I open my mouth, but no words come out. If LaMarcus had lived would I have been valedictorian? Would I have been an FBI agent? Or would I have been managing a CVS like my mother.

"It wasn't worth his life," I say.

Aji nods. "And that is why you *should* be angry."

Did LaMarcus die for me? I picture his young face, looking up at me. I see him trusting me, his superhero of an older sister. And then I break apart. Sobs overwhelm me. Huge wracking cries. Aji reaches out. He lays his hand lightly on my shoulder, offering me some tiny bit of comfort.

The pastor used to do the same.

I'm thrust back to my childhood Bible lessons in the pastor's little church. We lived in a dangerous world, and so our pastor brought us a Bible that matched it. Even as children, the pastor told us that Abraham had lost his brother. Abraham knew pain. That was why he could not accept the destruction of Sodom and Gomorrah without resistance. And Moses? Moses kept pleading with G-d and Pharaoh to stop the destruction of Egypt. He resisted G-d's plan. He could not

73

accept it. But Abraham and Moses were chosen by G-d as leaders. The pastor told us to question. He told us to think and to challenge. He didn't tell us simply to accept.

He told us that G-d wants leaders who push back.

"I believe you've been chosen," says Aji.

"I don't want to be chosen." I whisper back.

Aji lets out a small chuckle, "Well, it seems like *everybody* is choosing you."

I wipe away the tears with my sleeves. His statement has broken the moment.

"What do you mean?" I ask.

"Your boss chose you. You're very young to head a task force."

"I know," I say, "He chose me because he believed I could understand you and get inside your head. Because of my religious background."

"That is only *part* of the story," says Aji, with the confidence of a man who knows. "Your boss read the same essay I read. Only he believed it. He thought you would hate me like you hated the pastor. He thought that hatred would fuel this investigation."

"He wasn't wrong."

"No, he wasn't."

The silence returns, for just a moment.

"How about you?" I ask, "Did you choose me?"

I want the answer to be yes.

Aji seems to hesitate before he answers. And then he says, "I created a test. I'm just happy that you were the one who passed it."

I look at him, wanting to know more.

"On Saturday, if somebody had asked, you would have said that you *might* have been willing to put your life on the line to do what is right. But today, that is your truth. It is the truth because, on Sunday, you stayed at the Bandshell even though your team had disappeared. You were in fear for your life, but you stayed. You are willing to risk your life for justice. It is now a fact."

"Yes," I say, "I need justice."

With that, the case rushes back into my mind. The fingerprints, the gas leak, the charred body. The 31 dead. The hundreds wounded. Then, afterwards, the fire in my apartment.

The man I'm facing is behind it all. He shares the pastor's magic, that gift for religious gab. That talent for creating some kind of personal thrill. But that is all and I have to remember it.

The pastor didn't mean to kill, but Aji did. At the least, Aji is protecting another who is behind the violence.

"Why would *you*, a killer, choose an angel of justice?" I demand, suddenly angrier than I know I should be.

Aji seems taken aback. Then, his breath almost ragged, he says, "Because *your* justice, one way or another, will set me free."

"I need to know about the hidden agent," I say, as if declaring my intent will make him tell me what I want to know.

He clears his throat, seeming to summon the distance I'm trying to establish. Then he says, "I am not the one to tell you, but my people will. Just tell them that you are ready to hear about Tangara."

I just stare at him, uncertain what has changed. Or what 'Tangara' means.

"Why are you giving me information now?" I ask.

"Because," he says, "You are ready to hear the answers to your questions."

I don't understand. Nonetheless, I stand up, my body aching from the hours in the chair. Aji doesn't move.

Seconds later I pull open the door and step outside the cell.

My whole team is assembled outside. They've been waiting for me. They see the triumph on my face and they ask, as the door closes behind me, "What did you learn?"

But I don't tell them. I still can't trust them.

Instead I say, simply, "I have to go back to Brooklyn."

75

Tangara

Wednesday – 6:00 PM

As Marshall Johnson pulls the SUV to the curb outside Aji's hotel, he looks at me one more time and asks, "Are you sure?"

"I'm sure," I say, smiling a bit too weakly.

I told him, as soon as we got in the car, that I was going to meet Aji's people – alone. Johnson argued that it was a dangerous and stupid move. But I knew it was the only move I had. Aji's people weren't going to tell Johnson about Tangara.

As I open the SUV's door, Johnson has one more question. A little grin on his face, he asks, "What should I do while I'm waiting?"

He asks it almost as if we'd gone to the mall and I'd abandoned him on a convenient bench.

"There's a great Jamaican folk art museum on 8th," I say.

"Really?" he asks.

"Yeah," I say, "Do you like Jamaican folk art?"

"Do you?"

"I wouldn't know where the museum was if I didn't."

"Then," Johnson says with a grin, "I guess I'll like it too."

I close the door to the SUV, and he pulls away.

'At least that is going well,' I think with a satisfied smile.

The hotel is another matter. Last time around, the parking lot was empty. This time, a crowd has gathered. They are staring at me. They recognize me and they aren't happy to see me.

I take a step towards the hotel and the familiar chant begins "Free Aji, Free Aji, Free Aji." It isn't a shout, just a quiet, threatening, drumbeat. Every decibel of it is intended just for me.

I keep walking towards the hotel, arm in a sling, bruised and bandaged. As if to accent the point being made, a huge African man emerges from the automatic lobby doors and stands in front of them. He just stares at me. The message is clear. Everybody knows who I am, and I am not welcome.

That doesn't stop me. I am the one willing to risk my life for justice.

The crowd lets me through. Nobody touches me or threatens me. But their eyes are full of anger and resentment and hate. I am responsible. I have locked up the great Aji.

It seems like minutes pass before I reach the door. The man standing in front of it has not moved. I look up at him and he looks down at me. He doesn't ask what I want. He just stands there.

"I want to speak to Der'nube," I say.

He doesn't move.

I pull out my badge, although he knows who I am. And I say, again, "I want to speak to Der'nube."

He doesn't move.

I think for a moment and then I stand up on my toes, drawing as close to him as a I can, and I whisper, "It is about Tangara."

The man's face wrinkles in confusion and then surprise. Then, he steps to the side and grasps me gently by my left elbow. Together, we step towards – and then through – the automatic doors.

There are other young African men there, gathered in the lobby. They exchange quick words in a language I don't understand and then the man holding my elbow guides me towards the elevators. All the others seem to join us, the twin elevators carrying us up to the top floor. Two minutes later, I find myself back in Der'nube's room.

This time, though, we aren't alone.

The men crowd into the small space. Instead of sitting on the bed, I'm positioned on the beat-up chair. All around me are the young men. Some sit on the bed, some lean against the wall. Der'nube leans over the small trunk at the end of the bed. Carefully, almost gingerly, he lifts off the African-patterned cloth that lays on top of it. He folds it, sits on the trunk and then lays the cloth across his lap.

I want to ask about the cloth, but I hold my tongue.

Whatever "Tangara" unlocked, there seems to be some sort of ritual behind it.

Finally, Der'nube speaks, "The man is a mystery to me. I have no idea why he thinks you're ready."

I don't say anything.

He pats the cloth on his lap. Then with a resigned shrug he says, "This was my mother's. She gave it to me right before I killed her."

I just stare at him. I can't believe I just heard what he said. The others are nodding though, their expressions dead serious.

"Aji," says Der'nube, "Rescued us."

"You killed your mother?!?" I ask, forgetting about Aji for the moment.

"Do you know how children were recruited into the Chosen People's Liberation Force?" he asks.

"No." I'd read some things about the group – they'd been in summaries of their asylum applications my team had assembled. They'd never really had any context around them though.

Der'nube continues, "The Chosen, that's what they were really known as, would show up in a village. Hundreds of boys with guns. The foot soldiers were maybe 8 or 10 years old. The commanders, 14 or 15. Anybody who resisted or ran or tried to go for weapons was instantly shot dead. Sometimes, just to increase the terror, we'd kill a few people randomly. We weren't there for *just* anybody or anything, though. We came for two reasons. The first was food. We would steal whatever food the villagers had. Whatever we couldn't take, we'd burn. One way or another, we'd condemn those villagers to starvation. More important than food, though, were the recruits. Young boys, a couple of years from puberty. Can you imagine how we made them fight for us?"

"No," I say.

Der'nube is gently working the cloth on his lap. His fingers move with a nervous energy.

"It was simple. Ingenious really. We'd assemble all the villagers together. Naturally, they'd form into family groups. We'd pick the first young boy – somebody who was far from the best of the specimens. We'd pull him aside and we'd put a gun against his head. Then we'd put another gun into his hand. And we'd tell him to shoot his parents. Almost every time, that boy would delay. He'd try to have excuses, to pretend he didn't know what he was doing with the gun. Something, anything, to avoid our command. So, in front of all the other boys and the other families we'd shoot the boy – in the head so it was as graphic as possible. Then we'd kill the entire family, in the same way. Then we'd move on to the next boy and the next family. Some would suicide, but we'd kill their families nonetheless. Soon enough, there would be tearful goodbyes and parents urging their children to do exactly what we asked. Some parents would steady their children's hands, holding the gun for them – just so that *somebody* would live. And they would. Sons would shoot their parents and they'd be inducted into the Chosen. As a reward, we'd let their siblings live."

"Is that what happened to you?"

"Yes. We saw them coming. We knew what they did. We knew that if we played games or tried to hide which children belonged to which families, they'd always work it out. My mother gave me this bolt of cloth, her own special weave. And she told me to listen and do what the Chosen asked. And when my turn came, I shot her and my father. My older sister was raped. My younger siblings were spared, although I doubt they survived. I became one of the Chosen."

I can barely believe what I'm hearing.

"All of you?" I ask.

All around the room, heads nod. I'd never really thought of these young men as victims, asylum applications or not.

"You did this to other children?"

Again, the heads nod. "I was one of the commanders," says Der'nube, "I did it hundreds of times."

Monsters again?

"Why?"

"That's where the genius comes in. Nothing is worse than a boy who turns on his family and his village. We were instant outcasts. We were hated and we could never return to the lives we'd had. On some level, I guess, the very act of recruiting others justified the decision we had made. Every time a new boy joined us, every time a new boy

79

made the same decision we had, we felt less guilty about what we had done."

"That isn't enough to drive you to kill, is it?"

"No, it isn't enough. It was only a part of the puzzle. There was a web that trapped us into that life. There was the simple fact of survival. If we didn't do what those above us commanded, we would be killed. All of the horror we'd been through would be for nothing. Our parents' lives would have been sacrificed for nothing. It wasn't just about survival, though. Those who refused orders, or failed to win battles, weren't simply shot, they were tortured for hours or days before they died. There was also physical dependence. We had access to easy drugs. Methamphetamines for battle and recruitment. Heroin for down times. They'd dull our awareness, and our pain. They'd make us dependent. They'd lock us in. The commanders themselves were addicts. But even that wasn't enough. The final tool was religion. It was the most important one of all. Our leader was the Prophet Mombuto Yogula. He'd come to the African highlands to build the Chosen. He explained to us that _we_ were Chosen by G-d. He explained that the villages we struck had been condemned by G-d. He'd quote from the Old Testament. He'd quote commandments to kill every male, to kill infants, to kill livestock. Most of all, he quoted from the story of Abraham, telling us how Abraham was commanded to leave his people and his family and all he loved behind in order to make a new nation. He said we were walking in the footsteps of Abraham – when we killed our parents, we were forging a new people, blessed by G-d. The Prophet would pick the passages he shared based on what he wanted us to do. Our victories, in our young minds, were enough to validate him. Nobody could challenge us. G-d Himself had blessed us. It all came together. Fear, dependency, desperation for life. And purpose, purpose that could justify the rest. That's what the Prophet had woven together."

The faces are all looking at me. There is no regret or anger. There just seems to be resignation to their collective past.

I suddenly draw a connection that sickens me. "And Aji? Do you just follow him because once you came here you had to find another murderous prophet?"

Der'nube inhales deeply.

"Agent Jackson, you could have found stories like ours just by researching the Chosen online. You could have decided that's why we're here. For all we knew, you already had. Tangara doesn't unlock that. Tangara tells you something you had no way of knowing."

"What?" I ask.

"Who Aji is."

"I know who he is. He's a runaway from California who somehow picked you people up in South Carolina before suddenly rising to national prominence on the back of his intimidation and racketeering gig."

Der'nube stands up then. "Aji was wrong, you're not ready."

Almost as one, the men start to file out of the room.

I try to think of something to say, to bring them back. Even if they're going to simply cover for Aji again, I want to hear how they do it. I can't come up with anything. So, I just beg. "Okay, okay – tell me what you think I've got wrong. Please."

Der'nube has already turned to leave. He looks back at me, a skeptical eye. Those with him pause.

"Aji said he chose me because I'm willing to die for justice. Give me a chance."

"You might be ready to die, but you aren't ready to listen."

What do they want from me? I don't know what to say. Then Der'nube asks a question: "Agent Jackson, why are you here?"

Answers run through my mind. To pursue justice? Because Aji told me to come? That's why I'm *here* – in this room. I know that answer. He does too. He has to be asking some bigger question. Like, why I am here – an FBI agent, on this case. Aji had his theories: the pursuit of justice for LaMarcus, SAC Miller thinking I'd be a righteous inquisitor of a supposed man of G-d. But the question could be even bigger, right? Why has everything come together to put me here?

Finally, I answer. "I... I don't know."

"Listening starts with being able to ask the right questions." says Der'nube.

"But I can never answer *that* question."

He continues, as if he hadn't heard me, "Listening continues with being willing to hear that you do not yet understand."

I nod, confused.

"I'll listen. I promise. I'll listen."

Der'nube considers. And then he takes his seat again. The others come back in.

"Agent Jackson," says Der'nube, once everybody is back in the room. "Aji was the one who saved us."

"How? He's from LA not Garubia?"

"Will you listen?"

I nod, obediently.

He continues, "As far as I know, Aji has broken US law only once. He's an illegal immigrant."

"No, his parents came here. He was born here. It all checks–"

"Listen!"

I stop talking.

"*Michael Abakar* is from Los Angeles. *He* ran away from the foster system. Aji is from Garubia. He came ashore on South Carolina's Outer Banks. On a lifeboat from a cargo vessel whose captain had given him passage. Aji met Michael and then found him a family that was missing a son. And, in return, Michael gave Aji his identity."

Is this possible? Have I been pursuing a phantom all this time? I decide not to argue, and just to ask.

"Did you know him before?"

"A good question. The answer is, yes."

"How long before?" I ask.

I think I already know the answer. Der'nube just confirms it, "I've known him since he was recruited by the Chosen."

Suddenly the image of Aji shooting his own mother comes into my head. I hear words from the interrogation.

I have seen evil you can hardly imagine. I have seen it flourish. And I have seen G-d stand by and do nothing.

"Were you actually there?"

This time isn't Der'nube who answers. It is another of the men. He is younger, maybe 20. He is rail thin with a gaunt face and sunken eyes.

"I was." This man's voice is deeper and softer than Der'nube's.

"What happened?" I ask.

I don't really want to know, but I know I need to.

"I was the one who held the gun against his head. He did what we asked. After he was recruited, he was the same as any other recruit. He cried. He called out for his mother. He tried to convince others to join him in some sort of escape. We were used to it all. We'd all done it. Everything was designed to break in new recruits, and if they couldn't be broken, then to destroy them. But Aji found another path."

I just wait.

"I was his squad leader," says another of the men. This man is younger than Der'nube but older than the man who recruited Aji. He's shorter and stouter than either one of them. "The other boys wanted the drugs. At most, it took a few days to get them hooked. But Aji resisted. He didn't rebel, though. He didn't refuse orders. But he didn't try to vanish either. It was strange, at first. When the time came to kill, *he* asked to be the one to pull the trigger. A week after we'd recruited him, he was a recruiter. That was, well, really really fast."

Der'nube steps in, "It might be hard for you to imagine, but there were boys who were *too* violent for the Chosen. They enjoyed killing so much they forgot about the Prophet. We killed at the direction of the Prophet, to accomplish what *he* wanted. Not for pleasure. Of course, we didn't reject or kill those who enjoyed killing. We often promoted them. But they could spin out of control. So, we kept a close eye on them. After all, they might have been serving their *own* sickness, and not the Prophet's."

"You were worried about Aji being one of those boys?"

The squad leader says, "Yes, so I told my commander about him."

Another man says, "And I passed it up the line."

Der'nube says, "Eventually they told me. When we raided the next village, I watched him. I watched Aji kill. Because of what I'd been told, I expected to see pleasure. An eight-year-old with a gun destroying lives. I expected to see eagerness and joy. But I didn't see any of that. I couldn't understand what I saw though. I decided to let him be."

The squad leader continues, "After Der'nube went away, I couldn't help but watch Aji. I watched as he killed. Bit by bit, there was a change. Not in him, but in those he killed. I've seen so many people die. When they face death, they will protest, they'll cry, they'll fight. Some will simply surrender. A precious few will hold their heads in some kind of victory. Not with Aji though. Step by step, he got to a point where everybody he killed acted as if they had some kind of victory. I can't even explain it today. It is like they died, with hope."

"None of us could understand it," says the man who recruited Aji, "It seemed different every time. Sometimes Aji would act with savagery that made his victims feel better than him. They died convinced of some kind of superiority. Most of the time though, it seemed like he raised himself up. People died knowing what *Aji* was doing had to be done. That they were a part of something bigger. But there was more. In actual fights, we all killed. But when we raided villages, Aji alone did the killing for squad. Each of us was only given 5 bullets for a raid, the Prophet didn't want rebellion. Aji would collect all the bullets and do all the killing. Only later did I realize he was saving us from that killing."

Der'nube says, "After we came here, I heard a story. During World War I, a soldier was being led to his execution because he froze in battle. He had shell shock, but it was considered cowardice in those days. He was screaming and crying and fighting and protesting. A General saw him. He spoke a few words to him, and the man was led to his execution calmly and with pride. The staff officers asked the commander what he'd said to the man. And the commander said: 'I told him that I knew his crime was not great but that his execution, by serving as an example, would strengthen all of France.' That soldier died with purpose. It seemed like Aji could share that same thought, but without saying a word."

"Then," says the man who recruited Aji, "He began to focus on us. We felt *chosen*. We'd felt chosen, of course. But we'd felt like we'd been chosen to be erased in the service of a madman like the Prophet. Aji changed that. With him, we felt chosen to be raised up in the service of something greater. Even if that something greater was absolutely powerlessness. We still followed orders. We still killed. We had no choice. Aji knew that. He told me once though that he thought our suffering was going to make us stronger. He made us see our weakness as a path to strength."

"He tried that trick on me," I say.

"You can see it as a trick but I saw him stand tall and raise others up in the midst of hell. It was more than a trick. Somehow Aji can find meaning in everybody around him and he can help them find meaning in themselves. And, he can lift them up."

"Even those who he killed?"

"Especially those he killed. I don't know how, but especially those he killed."

I can hardly imagine such a thing.

The squad commander continues, "We couldn't help it. We followed our orders and our commanders, but Aji became our *leader*."

"And then," says Der'nube, "He was overheard by an ambitious young man. Aji was talking quietly with one of the boys who had fallen into his orbit. Aji was condemning the Prophet as an evil man. Word got to me and I told the Prophet. Normally the Prophet would have just killed such a boy, but he was curious, he wanted to meet him first. So, I brought Aji to the Prophet."

Der'nube pauses, like he's uncertain how to continue.

"And then?" I ask.

"I'm not sure you're going to be able to believe this part. I was there and I could barely believe it."

"I believe you said something about being willing to hear that which you can't understand."

Der'nube tips his head towards me.

"Okay... We were in scrubland. There were trees here and there but most of the land was dry. The villages were pretty far from one another. The Prophet was sitting on a chair. We used to carry it everywhere for him. All the top commanders were standing around him. He was sitting on his chair and he had his gun in his hand. It wasn't gold or ivory or anything like that. It was incredibly practical. It was a Russian submachine gun that shared parts with the AK-47. The Prophet's body was encircled with massive magazines full of bullets. It was like he wanted to be able to single-handedly put down a rebellion at a moment's notice. We all knew how this would end. He'd meet Aji, he'd ask him a few questions and then he'd kill him. When we moved on, we'd leave his body where it had fallen."

I interrupt, "Did Aji kill the Prophet?"

Der'nube continues as if I hadn't said a word. "Aji's face was hooded. Not for secrecy, everybody knew where the Prophet was. It was covered to shame him. I brought him in front of that throne, pushed him down on his knees and then pulled off the hood. Aji looked up then, straight at the Prophet. He didn't say a word. It was the Prophet who reacted. He opened his eyes wide and they began to shine with an intense light. I remember looking behind me to see if something was being reflected, but it wasn't. The Prophet's eyes were shining. Then the Prophet said, 'Those who bless you will be blessed and those who curse you will be cursed.' A moment later, the Prophet pushed his gun up below his own mouth and, a moment after that, he pulled the trigger."

Der'nube pauses.

"Agent Jackson, I *saw* prophecy. The only true prophecy I've ever seen."

He's right, I can't quite believe what he's telling me.

"There was chaos afterwards. The boy who had reported on Aji was killed almost immediately. But Aji's band formed up. They rescued Aji, none of them were hurt. When they fled, I followed them. They didn't trust me, but I knew what I'd seen. I had to bless Aji in some way, if I wanted to be blessed. The little band – these 14 people you see with me – came to a village. The villages cursed them and hit them and chased them away. They were pariahs. Aji's little band camped outside the village. They went hungry. That night another little band from the Chosen came to the village. They spent the entire night raping, pillaging and ultimately slaughtering the villagers."

Aji's little band moved on. They travelled further this time, gleaning what little food they could from the countryside. When they came to the next village, Aji went on alone. He walked in, a solitary boy, and they welcomed him. Within an hour the others were welcome too. I watched from outside the village. That night, on a midnight walk, Aji saw me and he brought me in to the village. The villagers were scared of me. I wasn't some young boy who'd been recently drafted. I was older. I was far more dangerous and far harder to redeem. But Aji convinced them to let me stay. He convinced *me* I was worthy of staying. We stayed for months. And those months, the villager's plants were unmolested by insects. Their animals were unharmed by predators. There was no sickness and the rains fell at the right times and in the right amounts. It was paradise. They knew we were the source of blessing and we knew that Aji was. They offered to bring us into their families. They wanted us to stay. But Aji refused. He had blessings to share with the world. He decided, in that village, to come to the United States. Whether people love it or hate it, nobody can escape the cultural footprint of the United States. Here, many more people could bless him and many more could be blessed.

"We left the village. We all applied for asylum at the US Embassy in Duomba. Miraculously, our applications were accepted – even mine. But Aji could not apply. Even in his brief time in Duomba people realized what he was. He faced no threats there. Businessmen, politicians, priests and everybody else who heard of him paid him homage. Even a cursory exam by the Embassy would have revealed that he was no asylum seeker. So... we came by air and he came by boat. A ship's captain blessed him with passage to a place off South Carolina's coast. Aji used a lifeboat to get to land.

"Aji had another reason for coming illegally, though. The name of that first village, the village destroyed by the remnants of the Chosen, was Tangara. Those who cursed Aji would be cursed. Aji didn't want Americans to think of him as a foreigner. He didn't want them to think of him as a killer. He needed to hide who he was. We all studied English intensely – he insisted on it. He even changed his accent, not an easy thing to do. He did it all because he needed to hide Tangara and everything that came before it. Because those who curse him are cursed and he came to bless."

I still don't believe in the reality Der'nube and the others seem to occupy. But *they* do. They care about his reputation. They clearly fear an actual curse.

"Why tell me then?"

"Because Aji told us to. He told you about Tangara."

I wait, hoping for some answer better than that one.

The recruiter adds, "Agent Jackson, it is one thing to be chosen. You can be chosen and not even know it. Most never do. It is another thing to realize you are chosen. Aji told you that you were. You understood that. You didn't really know what it meant though – to be chosen by Aji. We knew what it meant because we saw Aji in hell. We saw him rise above the reality of the Chosen. You just thought he was a runaway from California. To understood what it means to be truly seen by Aji, you have to know who Aji is."

The squad leader adds, "And you'd only be able to hear who Aji is from somebody *other* than him. If he'd told you this, it would have been impossible to believe."

"I've been chosen, then," I say. "What for?"

There are shrugs all around.

Der'nube says, "Maybe your job is about more than you think it is?"

"What could be more important than justice for the murdered?"

"Maybe," says Der'nube, "You know exactly what your job is, but need to understand just how important it is."

"Der'nube," I say, "I've followed every lead. I've chased every clue. I've spent a year trying to crack *this* case. What more could I do?"

Der'nube only pauses for a second before he says, "Listen."

The word hits me across the face.
Listen.
Be able to ask the right questions.
Be willing to hear that you do not yet understand.

Whether it is mysticism, divine intervention or the skilled manipulations of Aji, I *have* been chosen. Whatever bond Aji holds over these men, whether he is a demon or an angel, it means *something* to be chosen by him.

I decide then that I will do something more than what I have already done.
Whatever else happens, I will listen.
I will listen, and perhaps I will learn.

Conspirators

Thursday – 8:00 AM

By the time I hear the gentle knocking on the door, I'm already awake. I'd been waiting for Marshall Johnson to wake me up. He probably has another iced coffee and another reassuring and protective smile.

A woman could get used to this.

The night before, he'd picked me up at the hotel in Brooklyn and driven me back to Manhattan. I'd been feeling amazing. The meeting with Aji's men left me imagining that a whole new world had opened up to me. I didn't want to talk about the case with Johnson, though. Instead, I asked him about the Jamaican Folk Art museum and, surprisingly, he really knew his stuff. He'd not only gone to the museum; he'd paid attention when he'd been there. I don't know if he was genuinely interested in Jamaican Folk Art or genuinely interested in me (although I kind of hope it's the latter). Whatever the reason, he'd made an effort and I'd enjoyed the conversation. He wasn't only attractive, he was smart.

I promised him that if we had the chance, I'd tell him about other museums in New York. I admitted, being an art history major, that I was a major museum junky.

When we got back to the office, he checked my burns and my break. His hands were as gentle as ever. He asked if I needed the bruises on my torso examined. I felt like saying yes. I would have liked him to unwrap me. Nonetheless, I demurred. It wouldn't have been entirely professional. Then, I closed myself into the secure office on the 23rd floor, lay down on my cot and went straight to sleep.

I'd woken up early, anticipating his knock. I wanted to hear it, from the very beginning. When it comes, at 8 AM sharp, I get up from the cot, slip on my shoes, and head for the door.

Just as before, US Marshall Johnson is waiting. Once again, he's smiling. Once again, he's got a coffee in a thick paper cup and a large paper bag in his hand. I can't help my smile. "Iced and every kind of bagel?" I ask.

"No," he says, "I bought the same iced coffee, but I only bought the bagels you actually ate the last time around."

He's attentive too.

We walk, together, to the conference room. The team is there again, gathered and ready to work.

"What'd you learn last night?" Clara asks, as soon as I step into the room.

I'd thought about the question the night before and I knew just what I wanted to share. Nothing is private, of course. I'm a criminal investigator who conducted an interrogation. Nonetheless, it seems like it'd be somehow wrong to share *everything* I learned.

"They opened up like never before. They told me about their experiences in Africa. They told me they're drawn to Aji because he makes them feel like they can be redeemed. I think the most important thing I learned is that the attacks and the killings are being driven by a third-party. I think that third-party may well be a young African male."

"Why?" asks Clara.

"We're watching Aji's men and Aji carefully. Neither could have planned, or possibly even ordered, the truck that hit me the day before yesterday. It was a complex operation. They had to know which route we'd take, they'd have to know we'd be driving instead of walking, they probably had to arrange the demonstration. Aji's men didn't pull that off. Somebody else did, somebody we *aren't* watching."

Bill Riley, the conspiracies specialist, asks, "That all makes sense, but why an African?"

"You had to be in the room to see it," I said, "But those young men have a special connection to Aji. They see him as a kind of savior. I don't know why exactly, but he has a really incredible ability to connect with people who've been through horror – maybe specifically African horror. Maybe it is something his father or mother told him. I don't know. But he's connected. So, I wouldn't be surprised if there are more of them. We know about 15 men who came over together. It is possible one or more *other* former child soldiers came over as well – but were never publicly associated with Aji."

"Hidden agents?" says Bill.

"Exactly. I want us to look at other young male immigrants from Garubia and neighboring countries – legal or illegal. I want us to see if there are credit cards, travel records or other evidence that can tie any one of them – or even a group of them – to the deaths and injuries."

Heads nod around the room.

Matthew Crass begins spouting off lists of databases he can access, and the others huddle around him beginning to define the criteria they'll use to narrow down the list of possible suspects.

I don't know if the theory will lead anywhere. I have no problem believing Aji could be a killer. If he truly believes that those who curse him are cursed, he may choose to 'protect' society from his critics by murdering them. But, based on what I heard, I don't think he'd have *others* do the killing unless he had to.

If at all possible, he'd do the killing himself.

At the same time, *somebody* did arrange for my apartment to burn and my armored truck to be T-boned by a delivery van. Between simple coincidence, divine intervention, and a hidden agent the last option seems like the most reasonable one to pursue.

Despite that, it isn't the angle *I'm* going to pursue.

I stand up from the conference table. My team's faces turn towards me.

"What's up?" asks Clara.

I don't tell her that I'd told Der'nube that I'd listen. I don't tell her that that started with being willing to ask the right questions.

Instead I just say, "I want to look into something else."

My team's faces are confused and concerned. But it doesn't matter. I have a question I need to answer: I need to know why John Buckner was different than all the other victims.

I don't tell them that, though.

Somehow, I know I'm meant to find the answer on my own.

Hunt

Thursday – 8:04 PM

The SUV is cruising down the Grand Central Parkway leading from Queens to Hunts Point. Agent Johnson is driving, his eyes attentively watching the road and continually scanning for threats. I glance at him, wondering what is going through his head. He must have some idea of what I'm doing. He must be curious. It must take tremendous self-control not to ask.

My laptop is open in front of me. Johnson had removed the wrap from my hands earlier in the day – I can *just* painfully control the rugged little machine with my left arm, the one that isn't broken. Layered in the different windows are my various attempts to understand what made John Buckner different. So far only one reality sticks out: Aji took unique risks in John Buckner's case. We never, in any other case, encountered Aji paying anybody off – much less being separated by only one intermediary from the death or injury being investigated.

Aji stuck his neck out, and it still unclear why.

The day's investigations have already established that John Buckner wasn't especially prominent or influential and examinations of his computers showed that he wasn't working on some big or embarrassing story. I went by the remains of his house in Queens, the Fire Marshall's report in hand. The only thing I learned was the Elvis might have been telling the truth. While he'd cut the gas line, the explosion had been triggered later and possibly remotely. The light in the kitchen, a computer-controlled smartlight, turned on. It apparently wasn't screwed in perfectly and it sparked, triggering the explosion. I hadn't paid attention to it before, but the FBI computer forensics team had looked into it and found nothing of value. They believed John Buckner himself probably turned on the light.

That aspect of John Buckner's death was more like the other cases – seemingly accidental and tremendously hard to trace.

Elvis, though? Elvis still bothered me. Why did Aji meet him, face to face, to pay him to kill? Why pick somebody who wasn't entirely reliable? And why do it when, as far as we could tell, he'd never done anything like that before?

I spend the entire day looking for answers to that question: reviewing reports, talking to forensic investigators, reading the entirety of John Buckner's published works. Nothing had turned up. Nothing set John Buckner apart from the others who had died. Nothing but the payoff itself. I wonder if maybe Aji had a disagreement with a hidden agent. Maybe the agent didn't think Buckner needed to die. Maybe Aji disagreed. I don't know why, though.

Nothing seems to set John Buckner apart.

Now I'm heading to Hunts Point itself – the site of that payoff. I'd been there before, but maybe this time – by listening - I'll learn something new.

Until then, though, I've got nothing else to review or to read. I've got no more buttons to press or leads to pursue. Reluctantly, knowing there's no purpose in keeping it on, I lower the lid on my laptop and turn my full attention to Marshall Johnson.

"How long have you been a Marshall?" I ask.

He glances at me, ever so briefly. He pauses in his answer.

"5 years," he says.

"Was that too personal a question?"

"I am trying to keep it professional, ma'am," he answers. There's a hint of humor in his voice.

"Trying?" I say.

A tight smile. Contained mirth.

"Trying," he says.

"Can I ask you a *very* personal question?"

He nods.

"What's your first name?"

His eyes flick over again. "First name?" he asks.

"I'm guessing it isn't Marshall."

"No, not Marshall."

Another smile.

"Should I just run through the most common names in America?"

"Can you?" he asks.

"James, John, Robert, Michael, William, David, Richard – stop me if I get it – Charles, Joseph, Thomas..."

"Any more?" he asks.

"Those are the 10 most common. I didn't memorize the list after that."

"Why'd you memorize it at all?"

"I thought it'd be helpful to have some idea of when a name is so common that it is of absolutely zero use in an investigation."

"Wow."

"So?"

"It is none of those."

"Can you tell me what it is?"

"Well, I am afraid that might be a little too personal."

We cross the short bridge from Queens to Randall's Island.

"Too personal?"

"Well, I could tell you later. But... now? Now, it wouldn't be terribly professional."

"Later as when you're no longer protecting me."

"That's right."

"Then you can get personal?"

"That's right."

"Then you would want to get personal."

"That's right, ma'am."

I smile and press my advantage.

"What if I need your name, though, professionally."

"Why would you need it?"

"Maybe there will be two Marshall Johnsons around and I'll need to call out for the right one."

"Despite it being a common name, I'm the only Marshall Johnson in the New York Office."

"It could be an inter-regional situation."

95

The man keeps driving. We cross an even shorter bridge into the Bronx. A full minute later, he says, "Okay, but only because you might need it. Professionally."

I sit in my seat, waiting.

"Diagoras," he says.

"Diagoras?" I say.

"It's Greek," he says.

"I figured that out," I say, "But it isn't anywhere close to the top 10."

He grins, "If it's any comfort, my parents named me John."

"John Johnson?"

"Yeah."

"I can see why you changed it. Why Diagoras?"

"He was an ancient philosopher, and the name is basically as far from John as you can get. Outside of work, I'm an interesting guy."

I nod and smile. I like that. Moments later, we take the exit to Leggett Ave. I put the laptop on the seat behind me. A few blocks after that, when we get to the street where Aji and Elvis met, I ask Johnson to let me out.

"By yourself?" he asks, concern once again in his voice.

"Nobody knows to expect me here, and I think you'll intimidate the heck out of any witnesses."

I give him a wink and a once-over as a consolation prize.

He nods, his smile broad.

"I'll be watching from afar," he says as he pulls to a stop.

"Kind of you," I say as I open the door and hop out. As the SUV pulls away, I know Marshall Johnson will park nearby. If I call, he'll be there to rescue me. For now, though, I take in my surroundings. The street I'm on is lined with walkup apartments and pavement broken through by patches of grass. There are small commercial establishments folded into the ground-floors of some of the buildings. A beauty salon, a bodega, a bar. We'd seen both Aji and Elvis enter this street, but the street itself doesn't have any cameras. The cameras in the bar and the bodega are inside-only and the beauty salon only has one on the cash register. A few of the apartment buildings have cameras, but, again, they're inside. They can't make out what's happening outside the buildings' doors.

We'd looked at every camera there was, of course. But we'd found nothing. Aji had either stayed on the street or gone to one of the apartments; he hadn't visited any of the businesses.

Nonetheless, it couldn't hurt to ask around a second time.

The Beauty Salon is the obvious first choice. It's closed, though. I walk over to the windows and glance in. It looks like any other beauty salon with one exception: there's a little photo of Aji in the window. There's a chance they know him. Maybe he had a key to the place. I decide to come back tomorrow to ask about that.

I head across the street to the bodega. The awning is lit up from behind. It displays the keywords a pedestrian might be drawn to. LOTTO, SANDWICHES, WIC & FOOD STAMPS, ICE CREAM. It looks like any other bodega in the city.

I pull out my phone one-handed (the arm in the sling isn't terribly useful) and open a picture of Elvis as I step into the little store. Aji is famous. *This* Elvis isn't. Despite the name, he's a non-descript, middle-weight, black, homeless guy. People need a photo of Elvis to know if they've seen him around.

I turn the phone in my hand as I approach the counter. There's a cashier sitting there, a rail-thin middle-aged Hispanic guy.

"Seen this guy?" I ask the cashier. He looks up from the show he's watching on a tablet computer. He takes a glancing look at my phone and says, "Yeah, Elvis."

I hadn't expected that.

"He a regular here?"

"Sure, up until a few weeks ago he came by pretty much every night. You a cop?"

"FBI."

"An FBI Agent interested in Elvis. Huh."

"Huh? Why Huh?"

"Oh, Elvis was a conspiracy nut. I guess a lot of homeless people are. He used to hang out in the magazine area and just read stuff. He didn't smell bad and he was good company, so I just ignored him. You know."

"I get it," I say, conversationally. "What kind of conspiracies was he into?"

"All sorts. Roswell, government antennas, 9/11 as an inside job. The whole gamut. One of his favorites, which is pretty funny with you here, is that the FBI was out to get him."

"Out to get him, how?"

"He claimed the FBI used to visit him. Tell him they'd kill him if he didn't do what they wanted. All sorts of crazy stuff. It wasn't just the FBI, though. He thought there were aliens in Hunts Point too. I guess I'd also think it was pretty interesting if you said you were from Alpha Centauri." He chuckles a bit.

"You ever see him with Aji Abakar?"

"*The* Aji? You know about that?"

"About what?" I ask, suddenly more excited.

"Well, Aji – when he's in town – would come up here. He used to walk by the store. Sometimes he'd stop in. He spent a lot of time in this neighborhood."

"*The* Aji Abakar?"

"Yeah, what other Aji do you know?"

"I don't know. It might be a pretty common Indian name."

"I'm talking about Aji Abakar. *The* Aji."

"Any idea why he came up here?"

"Nope. Maybe he has a girlfriend on the block or something," another chuckle.

"Why's that funny?"

"It's just kind of hard to imagine Aji with a girlfriend, you know?"
I don't.

"So... a boyfriend, then?"

"No, no, nothing like that. It's hard to imagine Aji finding somebody who has enough in common with him to have, you know, a *real* relationship. Love him or hate him, he's pretty unique."

"I get that," I say. Even his relationship with Der'nube and the rest of the former Chosen is hardly normal.

"He ever meet Elvis?" I ask.

"Not that I saw. I mean, they could have run into each other. But I never saw it. I do know Elvis *never* talked about him. And Elvis would talk about *everything*. It was strange, having Aji in the neighborhood and Elvis not even noticing."

"Maybe he was trying to pretend he didn't know him because the two of them were up to something together."

"Elvis?" the cashier laughs. "He could have used a little blessing, but he wasn't a terribly reliable kind of guy. I can't imagine him being in cahoots with anybody. I wouldn't be in cahoots with him and *my* standards aren't terribly high."

"Would Elvis have told you if they were up to anything?"

"Maybe, but I don't think so. Elvis talked about a lot of things, but he was real private about his own situation."

"Except when the FBI visited him."

"You think that was real."

"No."

"So, there you go. He was real private about his own *reality*."

I can't think of any more questions, not right now. I thank the man and ask him to give me a call if he figures out anything else. Then I buy a Snickers, picking it up and paying with my one good hand. I find people are more helpful if they feel like you've given them something, and not just taken up their time.

A moment later I'm back outside the store. There's only one place left, the bar. I walk down the street, taking the place in. It is a rundown establishment named "The Railroad Lounge." I'd been there before. It has no posters promising live music, there's just a few neon ads promising cheap beer and booze. It is *not* a classy establishment.

I push open the door. As my eyes adjust to lighting that somehow seems dimmer than that of the nighttime street, I remember the distinct décor of the place. Whoever built it tried to stick with a theme. An actual railroad track runs up the wall. A door from of an old boxcar takes up an entire wall. The bar itself is made up of railroad ties laid out in rows and covered in plexiglass. Antique railroad signal lights hang over the bar, provided a distinct glow to the whole place.

The neighborhood is known as a nexus for distribution and logistics operations. Rail lines used to run out from here to places all over the city. I guess the bar's owners glommed onto that. They put a lot of effort, and very little money, into making the place unique.

There's one other customer in the bar. I take a seat as far from him as I can manage. The bar stools are train wheels mounted on railroad ties and covered with plexiglass. The stools aren't terribly comfortable, but they fit right in with everything else.

I order a beer.

The bartender, an older white guy with a scruffy face, slides one over. I know him. I'd interviewed him during the initial investigation. I show him my phone, with the photo of Elvis on it.

"Hello again," I say.

"Hi," he says.

"Can you tell me again what happened, you know, the night I was asking about before."

"Nothin'," comes the reply, "Nothin' happened. It was a normal night. Aji didn't come in here, or that other guy. You have the video tapes."

"Yup," I say, sipping my beer, "I was just curious if you'd remembered anything else."

"Nope," says the bartender.

I go back to sipping my cheap beer.

"You ever seen Aji?" I ask.

"Nope," he says, again.

I nod. Aji must have been visiting one of the apartments. Or conducting some business in the closed beauty salon.

The other customer is at the other end of the short bar. Unexpectantly, the bartender leans in close to me.

"I doin' okay, right? I don't got nothing to worry about, right?"

I look straight into his eyes. There's fear there, mixed with some measure of hope. It's like he's appealing to me for his own safety.

"What do you mean?" I ask. Is the bartender following some kind of script?

"You know... I don't want to say because, you know..."

He's following a script, and he's scared?

"Ah, of course," I say, "The other guy."

I give him a wink.

"Yeah, because of the other guy," the bartender says.

"Yeah, I'm just checking up on you," I say, "You're doing great."

"Whew," says the bartender. He shakes himself and smiles deeply. A moment later, though, the smile disappears.

"What's wrong?" I ask.

"Oh, I dunno. It just don't feel right. And I can't tell nobody why. Is it okay if I talk about it with you? I mean, I won't get in any trouble, right?"

"No trouble," I say, raising my hands in mock salute. "I'll do whatever I can to make it easy for you to do what you need to do."

I'd never had a bartender confide in me before.

The guy seems a bit nervous. He bites his lip.

Then he says, "Do we really have to do this?"

I think about asking, "Do what?" but he thinks I know. Maybe he'll think I'm setting him up for some kind of trap if I play stupid.

"I'm afraid so. It's important." I say.

"Yeah, that's what the other guy said. But it just don't feel right."

"Why not?"

"Well, I know you guys told me Aji is a killer and all. But... I'm just not seeing it."

"He has that effect on a lot of people."

"Yeah, but they don't know him like I do."

"What do you know that's different?"

"He talks to me, you know."

I don't say anything.

"I don't really want to break his confidence."

"Bartender-drinker privilege?" I ask.

"Something like that. I mean, sometimes that can be like a holy thing. It was with Aji."

"Holy? How?"

"He used to come here, whenever he was in New York. He'd be wearing a hat pulled down low. Most people probably wouldn't of

101

recognized him. He'd sit in the corner and he'd order drinks. He'd get really drunk. But he didn't want people to know he was here, so I pretended not to notice who he was. After a few months, well, he started talking to me. You know?"

I nod, briefly. Then I just wait. People like to fill silence.

"He told me things. He said he came up here to drink because he had to pretend to be tougher than he was – because those around him couldn't see him being weak. He couldn't really handle it though. The stuff he went through. That's why he got drunk like he did. I mean, he wasn't drinking to forget. He was drinking to hurt himself. He hated himself. He told me he felt like people died *because* of him. He claimed that they were cursed because he couldn't be good enough for them to bless him. I mean, I felt he didn't tell this stuff to nobody. But he was telling me. The man was good. I mean, I know a lot of low-lives – comes with the territory. This guy was no kind of low life. I just don't think he deserves to be set up."

He pauses, looking to me for some kind of judgment.

I can't let the bartender know what I'm thinking. I'd never really thought Aji was *hurt* by the death and injury that seemed to follow him. Or that he'd be ashamed by it; so ashamed that his own men couldn't know what he was going through.

If there is a hidden agent, then Aji might also be his victim.

I keep playing my role, acting as if I'm a part of what's going on.

"We do *know* he's guilty," I say.

"Well, I didn't want to do it. Okay. I didn't see that part of him. I know you guys only wanted me to do one small thing. But I can tell you, I wouldn't of done it – even though y'told me it was important."

He pauses. Then says, "Truth is, I only did it cause that other guy told me he'd kill me if I didn't."

Kill him?

The bartender continues, "You know, the other guy said he could make the evidence look like I attacked him. He told me the medical examiner was a good friend. He said he did it whenever he needed to. But that he didn't want to do it to me. You guys *can* do that, right?"

"Of course we can," I say.

"Yeah. This country is screwed. Anyway, he said all I needed to do was do what he asked and tell the story right, for whoever asked about it afterwards. Then I'd be okay. You came in, twice, and I told it right. So, I'll be okay, right?"

"You sure did," I say. "What actually happened, though? You know, because you've never told *me* that."

"Oh. It was a simple thing. The other guy came in and asked me to keep Aji's bills separate. He said he'd pay me for them. One night, while Aji was here, he came in and picked up the money. Paid me for it fair and square. I asked him if he wanted me to erase the video surveillance or anything and he said it'd already been taken care of. And that was it."

It all clicks together. Aji's bills had been saved. With fingerprint and DNA evidence on them. The cash used to pay Elvis had been planted. To make it work, the bartender was threatened. Elvis was too. Elvis Brown may have cut the gas line, but he didn't want to.

Aji didn't know anything about any of it.

Somebody else made it seem like he had.

But who?

SAC Miller was the one who suggested we fingerprint the bills.

"You see me on TV?" I ask, hoping to draw out some revealing comment.

"Yeah," says the bartender. "It's weird that you can kill whoever you'd like, but you can't control a crowd of peaceful protestors."

There's a hint of bitterness in his voice.

"Yeah," I say.

Just then the guy at the other end of the bar lays a few bucks on the counter and gets up to leave. The bartender doesn't say anything more. The TV gambit didn't work.

I say, "You know, the FBI has a lot of bureaucracy. We gotta file reports on everything, even the 'off-the-books' stuff, if you know what I mean."

"Yeah," says the bartender, uncertainly.

"I wasn't really sent here to check on you. I was sent here to double-check the people who set this all up."

"Okay…"

"So… I need to know which 'other guy' visited you. We got a lot of them. It's for my report, you know?"

"Uh, yeah. It was that older white guy you were on TV with."

"SAC Miller?"

"Yeah, that's what the TV said."

"Well that checks out with our records. And you told your story perfectly. I know you feel bad about Aji, but we're doing what's best, I assure you."

"Okay," says the bartender, still sounding uncertain.

Then he glances up and towards the door. His eyes widen in complete panic. I don't know what's happening, but almost instinctively, I push up with my left arm and vault over the bar. The sound of the shot in the enclosed space is deafening.

Another rings out as I clear the bar, safely ducking behind the thick iron railroad ties. I look up and see the bartender falling to the ground in front of me, his eyes still open in shock. He hadn't even had a chance to scream.

For a moment, I stare at the lifeless body. It is the first time I've seen someone killed since LaMarcus.

What in the heck is going on here?

I pull my gun with my left arm. I keep it chambered. There's no need to pull back the slide with my broken right arm.

Quickly, I dart to a spot farthest from the door. Then I pop up, gun aiming towards the door. Then I see him. Marshall Johnson, with *two* guns in his hands.

Marshall Johnson?

Protective Marshall Johnson?

I don't hesitate. I aim, single-handed, and fire.

All I hear is a click.

Confused, I crash back towards the floor behind the bar. There's another boom in the confined space; another gunshot. A bottle explodes, right behind where I'd been standing.

Special Agent Johnson is trying to kill me? My gun doesn't work? Why doesn't my gun work?

I look behind the bar, for anything I can fight back with.

I see a wooden bat. It seems weak, surrounded by the iron ties that make up the bar. Unlike them, though, it isn't welded to anything else. I grab it and then begin to move *extremely* slowly from my position. I move towards where Johnson had been, closer to the front of the bar. The floor is made up of old wooden boards, it is very hard not to let to squeak. As I move, I listen.

I can hear Marshall Johnson moving. He isn't as careful as me. He knows he's armed and he knows I'm not.

When I hear him directly across from me, I rise upwards already swinging the bat with my left arm. I put all of my aching body into the swing. His gun is up, but it's aiming at where I had been, not where I am now. He moves, adjusting his aim. But the bat moves faster. He squeezes the trigger on his pistol a moment before the bat connects. I feel a sharp pain as the bullet grazes my right arm. My swing continues, the bat connecting, hard with his head.

He tumbles down. I don't know if he's dazed, unconscious or dead.

I stand there for a second, uncertain what to do. Then the realization hits me: I'm unarmed and I'm very very alone.

I do the only thing I think I can do.

I run.

Run

Thursday – 11:00 PM

Run. That's the first thought that goes through my head. My second thought is that I am *good* at running. I could have been a college athlete. If running is all I need, then I'll be fine.

But my third thought is that I'm no super spy. I passed my qualifications at Quantico. I can shoot, which would matter if I had a gun. I can run, but I don't know where to run to. And I can follow procedure, but there aren't any procedures for this.

I don't even know what *this* is.

I see an ATM. Cash suddenly seems like a very good idea. I veer over to it, pull out my bank cards and withdraw as much as I can. $400 from each account and $1000 in cash from my credit cards.

As the bills flit out of the machine, I realize that Marshall Johnson somehow heard the bartender. Otherwise, he wouldn't have known to barge in. He wouldn't have known to kill the bartender, or me. Somewhere on me there's a microphone. Maybe even a locator. The cash is new, though. The cash is safe.

Standing right there, I drop my wallet and cell phone on the ground. I almost hope it is stolen – people using my credit cards all over the city will make it harder to find me. I take off my sling, gingerly. Then I take off my jacket, wincing with the pain. The arm is covered in blood.

I leave it all there, on the ground.

I can't take off everything though. I need new clothes.

I glance around, but I don't see anything that could help. So, I stuff the money in my pocket and I start to run, again.

A few blocks away I see a thrift shop, the kind that sells second-hand clothes. It's closed. I try to jimmy the door, but nothing happens. I need new clothes, though. I take out my useless gun and smash the glass door. I reach through and open the door from the inside.

106

Security isn't great at second-hand clothing stores.

There is an alarm though. It starts blaring almost immediately.

I burst through the door. I reach the first rack and pull of the first clothes that seem like they might be large enough for me. Then I pull $200 out of my pocket and drop it in the floor. I don't need something that suits me well. I just need something that can cover me up.

Seconds later, I dash back out of the store.

A half a block later, I duck between buildings. As quickly as I can, given my arm, I strip out of my holster, my shirt and my pants. I rip a part of the shirt off and tie it around my arm, to staunch the bleeding. I wonder how much I should take off. I decide on everything. I just leave it all on the ground and I grab the clothes I'd stolen.

I hadn't grabbed a shirt and pants though. I hadn't even grabbed a dress or a skirt. I'd grabbed some long bolt of cloth. I struggle to put it on, trying to wrap it around myself. I don't succeed. In the dim light of the alley, I try to look more closely at what I'd stolen.

I see a pattern, and I realize I have an African robe just a little like the one Der'nube's mother had given him.

I try to remember the pictures from school and the images I'd seen in various museums. Then I try again, wrapping the cloth around myself in the closest approximation to what I'd seen before. I know it isn't right, but at least the clothes aren't just falling off.

I'm ready to leave now, but do I take my gun? Even a gun without a firing pin can scare people. But the only people I need to scare will know that the pin is missing.

I'll lose the gun.

I look at it closely though, before I toss it aside. It is a Sig Sauer P320, just like mine. It weighs the same. It feels the same. It probably has the same ammunition. I wonder if it is my gun, just disabled. Then I look at the side of the receiver, expecting to see the familiar serial number stamped onto it. The serial number, though, has been rubbed out. This is a black-market weapon. That's when it hits me. Johnson had *two* guns. One was probably mine. Ballistics will show that *I* killed the bartender.

That sobering thought in mind, I wipe the black-market gun clean with the remainder of my shirt and drop it in the alley. I emerge, with $1,600 and some clothes I know I'm not wearing quite right.

I have no idea how much time I have left before Johnson and whoever he's working with figure what's happened. I have no idea how much time I have until they catch up with me. I do know the resources they have at their disposal. They can track my phone. I've gotten rid of that. They can track my credit cards, but they're gone too. The next thing is cameras. Cameras all over the city loaded up with facial recognition systems. I have to deal with the cameras.

I see a pharmacy that's open. I step inside and buy cotton balls, putty, makeup, a new sling, gauze and a hat. My purchases complete, I head to the restroom.

The sling and gauze are for my arm. I tuck the cotton balls into my mouth, above my teeth. They'll change the shape of my jaw, so the facial recognition systems won't recognize me – at least not as easily. I use the putty to change the shape of my nose and eyebrows. Finally, I apply the makeup to make it all look *somewhat* realistic.

The hat goes on last, so the store's cameras won't capture my new appearance. When I walk outside, I'm a new woman. I'm not just black, but African. My clothes hang reasonably well, and my facial features are more prominent than they've ever been. It might just be enough for me to hide.

A few blocks later I walk past another bar. I see the TV inside. SAC Miller is on it. I stop and watch for just long enough for him to explain that one of his agents, Special Agent Neisha Jackson, killed a witness who was going to testify against Aji Abakar. As he explains it, the FBI believes Special Agent Neisha Jackson took a bribe from Aji Abakar's organization and then earned her fee by killing an innocent man. Thus, Special Agent Neisha Jackson is a dangerous fugitive from justice. My picture, from my badge, is flashed up on the TV.

I walk away from the bar. I can't lurk anywhere for too long. Everybody will be looking for me.

Somehow, I've got to figure out what's going on and who is ultimately behind it.

Night

Friday – 1:00 AM

The night is remarkably calm as I walk. The moon is full, and the stars shine in a cloudless sky. The air seems crisp and clean, freshly blown in from some place other than New York City.

As I walk, I realize that I'm *not* running. I'm not heading north. I'm not leaving the city and trying to escape. I'm heading towards Harlem and after that Lower Manhattan. Or even Brooklyn. Without even thinking about it, I'm heading towards trouble.

I need to figure out what I'll do once I get there.

I begin to sort things out in my head. As I walk, putting one step in front of the other, my thoughts form into theories and the beginnings of answers.

I know my gun was replaced. The only time it could have happened was while I slept. My 'secure' overnight room wasn't secure. At some point, when I was exhausted from my injuries, Johnson – or somebody else – snuck in and replaced my gun. They took the firing pin out of the weapon they gave me. They disarmed me without me even knowing it.

Why, though?

I ask myself what I know? I know SAC Miller set up Aji. He could have done it because he was tired of the case not progressing. He could have done it to protect the innocent lives of future critics. It would be understandable. Criminal, but understandable. Almost like the idea that Aji had been killing detractors because he honestly believed he was protecting people by doing so. Or a mentally ill man killing people he believes are demons.

With this theory, SAC Miller hadn't meant to kill the bartender. He hadn't wanted to, until the man revealed his secret to me. Like a man covering a small fraud with a huge one, SAC Miller had killed the bartender when the bartender had threatened not only his case but his career.

The idea makes sense, except for one element: Marshall Johnson. US Marshall Johnson isn't in the FBI. He wouldn't have been frustrated by the case. He hadn't known about it until a few days ago, right? It was US Marshall Johnson who pulled the trigger, not SAC Miller. It was US Marshall Johnson who tried to kill me.

Is that the only reason why he'd flirted with me? To slow me down? To catch me off-guard if he needed to attack me? Was he just trying to get to know me better so he could keep track of what I was looking into and what I was learning?

I can't help it, but I find myself hoping that he had been genuinely interested in me. At least, up until the point where he tried to kill me.

Why was Johnson involved? Whatever it was that triggered the bartender's death, it wasn't just frustration with the case.

I think back to my interview with Aji. Aji had said I was chosen by SAC Miller. Not because of my expertise, but because I would be vengeful in my pursuit of Aji. I'd be single-minded in my desire to bring down a so-called Holy Man.

That's why I'd been selected. That has to be the motivation behind everything I've seen. I hadn't paid much notice to it, but when he'd first suggested I take over the case, SAC Miller himself had said that if people started believing in Aji's so-called miracles, the remarkable social advancements of modern America would be completely undermined. Reason would be replaced with blindness. I'd agreed with him, but left it at that.

I suppose he might have been waiting for something more. Maybe he was inviting to whatever group he and Johnson belong to; a group willing to break the rules in an effort to protect society from men like Aji.

It explains why SAC Miller *wanted* publicity. He wanted to destroy Aji publicly, while dragging his character through the mud. He wanted the press conference. He wasn't going to retreat because for him the whole point had been to show the power of the state.

I'd simply been his tool.

I'd been a useful tool. From the beginning I'd believed that Aji had to be guilty – and that all I needed to do was to find the evidence to put him away. Of course, I don't know that Aji *isn't* guilty. He is able to kill. Perhaps the delusion of a curse has driven him to do so. Even the bartender's story doesn't rule that out. Nonetheless, I do know he did *not* kill John Buckner.

I wonder why Miller and Johnson hadn't used a real insider. Why rely on me, a somewhat unknown quantity? The press conference, again, provides the answer. A reporter had asked whether I was chosen because I was a young black woman. Maybe that was part of the character assassination. They wanted to destroy a young, up and coming, black man. Who could do that more completely than a young, up and coming, black woman? No charges of racism would taint the accusations. It hurts, but they'd chosen me not only because I had an axe to grind, but because I was a young black, inexperienced, female agent.

They figured I'd be easy to manipulate. And up until a few hours ago, they'd been right.

I walk across the bridge into Manhattan, seeing the water lazily float beneath me in the boxed-in Harlem River.

That's why Johnson had gotten involved. They'd gotten worried after my first interview with Aji. I'd emerged angry, worried that Aji's concern was simply a threat. But they'd seen another possibility – that I'd see that concern for what it was.

They knew that they needed insurance.

That's why Johnson had been assigned to me.

He was there to kill me if I learned too much.

Who had suggested him, though? Was it Clara or Miller?

Is Clara also involved?

I can't exactly remember.

As I keep walking, I realize how little I actually know. I know Johnson and I know Miller. Maybe Clara too. But who else is part of the conspiracy? Other members of my team? Others even higher up in government? Beat cops?

I'm being pursued and I have no idea who my enemies actually are. There must be more though. Miller had told the bartender the Medical Examiner would find what he wanted him to. That had to be true. Otherwise, whatever had just happened at "The Railroad Lounge" couldn't be covered up. A competent investigator would know I wasn't alone with the bartender when he was shot.

The conspiracy must be huge. I just don't know how huge.

I keep walking, glancing nervously – waiting for a nightmare to come rolling down the street in a dark SUV. I don't see any dark SUV's though.

The conspiracy continues to grow in my mind. Elvis cut the gas line. The smart house turned on the light in the kitchen. Who, though, unscrewed it just the right amount? Who triggered the smart house?

The press conference answers that question as well.

A team had been sent to assess John Buckner's security. That same team must have unscrewed the lightbulb. Whoever was on it, at least one of them is involved.

How the hell am I going to survive this?

As I cross 110th street, exhaustion suddenly overcomes me. I feel completely overwhelmed. There is no light at the end of this tunnel and I've already been through a high-risk arrest, an apartment fire, a near-riot, a car accident and a shooting. Now I'm trying to hide myself as I walk the streets of New York – the most surveilled city in America. All of which says nothing about my conversations with Aji and my realizations about LaMarcus.

I'm exhausted. I need to rest. But I don't know where.

I could go to a public park. But if the police see me, they won't just roust me. They'll report me and somebody will arrange for me to disappear.

How about my old apartment? I can walk the 30 or so blocks to that burned out husk, but I'm sure it is under surveillance.

It isn't worth the risk.

Some random rooftop? I might be able to slip into a building, but it's unlikely at two in the morning. People tend to be suspicious at two in the morning. They might call the police or FBI. Even if I get into a building, roofs tend to be locked. A rooftop isn't worth the risk.

I just keep walking, the exhaustion rising unstoppably.

I stop thinking. I just keep moving. Literally one step at a time.

Up ahead, I see a middle-aged black woman in scrubs. She's walking towards me. I ignore her, but she doesn't ignore me. She walks right up to me, blocking my path. I pull to a stop. I'm too tired to run from her. If she called for help, I'd never be able to get far enough to matter. In that moment, I realize that I've already surrendered. All those who stood with me have abandoned me.

The conspiracy *will* overwhelm me. It is inevitable.

I can't begin to fight back.

I can't even run anymore.

I see a name tag on the woman's shirt. It reads "Dr. Abade".

As she stands there, she looks me up and down. I'm about to be identified and there's nothing I can do about it. I mean, I could hurt her – but for what? She doesn't deserve to be hurt just because she's doing what she thinks is right and I probably wouldn't get far anyways.

Instead I just stand there, passively, awaiting my fate.

Then she says, "Dear child, you're wearing that all wrong."

"What?" I ask, suddenly confused.

She chuckles. "Oh, and you are no kind of killer."

I let Dr. Abade lead me up and into her apartment. She bandages the place where the gunshot grazed my skin. She examines my break and my burns. She feeds me. And then she lays me down in her bed. She explains that she'll take the couch.

I'm exhausted but I'm not worried that she'll call the police. I know she could have done that without stopping to help me.

Today has brought fear and tomorrow will bring terror. Right now, though, I am at peace.

Just before I close my eyes, I find myself thanking G-d for Dr. Abade.

Collection

Friday – 8:00 AM

I am exhausted, but I don't sleep well. The image of the bartender falling keeps running through my mind. I imagine that Johnson didn't miss me. That I'm laying there, alongside the bartender as SAC Miller's forensic investigators create their stories. I watch my body from over their shoulders, watching them bend what they see to fit the narrative they need.

Then, I dream that I'm lying on the floor of my 'secure' FBI office. I smell coffee and fresh bagels. I open my eyes. I see the sterile gray of the office ceiling. And then Marshall Johnson steps into view. He's standing over me, pointing my own gun at my face.

He pulls the trigger.

I scream, sitting up in a sudden panic.

Johnson isn't there, though. I'm on Dr. Abade's bed. The ceiling isn't a sterile gray, but an earthly yellow. Reddish curtains filter the light from outside. I'm safe.

I smell it then. Fresh coffee and bagels. They aren't a source of threat and danger, though. They are a source of safety and security.

A moment later, Dr. Abade appears in the doorway to the bedroom. She looks in, her face kindly and concerned.

"Are you okay?" she asks. She has a slight West African accent.

"Yes, yes. Just a bad dream," I say.

She nods, knowingly.

I get up from the bed. The sheets are wet with my sweat. "I can change these," I say.

"No need," she says, "I can manage it."

I stand up.

"Come to the kitchen, I've got some breakfast for you."

I get up and go to the restroom. Then I follow her down the cozy hallway. The floors are decorated with the geometric patterns of West African weaving. The walls are decorated with tapestries and masks. I follow her into the tiny kitchen. The appliances are shiny and new, but little pottery containers line the surfaces. The room smells most strongly of chilis. However, laid out on the little table, are a pair of coffees and a small bag of bagels.

I somehow doubt this is Dr. Abade's usual breakfast.

I take a seat at the small table.

"Why did you help me?" I ask.

Dr. Abade selects a coffee and passes it to me. "I saw the news. I thought you might have done what you're accused of. When I walked up to you last night, in the street, I looked at your face and... I saw myself. I just knew you weren't guilty."

"You saw yourself?"

Dr. Abade inhales deeply.

"I had to run once," she says.

I nod, pretending I know what she's talking about.

I take a sip of the coffee.

"What now?" I ask.

"I figure that I'll help you with your disguise. Maybe you can hide here until you figure something out."

I think about that for a minute, opening the bag of bagels.

"No," I say, "They aren't trying to arrest me. They're trying to kill me. I would appreciate your help on my disguise. But then you need to send me on my way. You can't hide me for long and the risks are just too high."

"I'm willing to try," she says.

"I'm not," I answer. "This story isn't going to end well."

I take a deep breath, and I know that I do need one more thing from her.

"You can do one very important thing for me, though." I say.

"What is that?"

"I need you to hear my story."

I think she understands. She says, simply, "I would love to."

So, we sit in that little kitchen and I tell her. I tell her about Aji and Johnson. About SAC Miller and the bartender. About Der'nube and the other child soldiers. I tell her about the fabric and the tragic story behind it.

115

As I speak, I realize how totally alone I am. I'm estranged from my mother and from my team. I'm cut off from any world I know. I'm running towards trouble, with no idea of what to do when I get there.

An hour or two must have passed before I come to the end of my story. The doctor reaches for one of the cupboards and pulls out a tablet computer. She types a few things into it. Then, she touches my hand gently.

"A young boy fell while running yesterday evening. I'm a plastic surgeon. That's why I was out last night. When this is all over, maybe you should thank him."

"What do you mean?" I ask.

"Come with me," she says.

She rises from her chair and walks back to a second bedroom. I follow her. There is no bed there, though. Just racks and racks of fabric and clothing. All have African patterns, bright, strong and geometric. The room is a blaze of design. Dr. Abade moves through the racks and then selects one garment and pulls it out. It is almost the same weave as Der'nube's. A near perfect match.

"Is this the cloth you saw?" she asks.

I nod, surprised.

"It is a Central African weave, from one of the Sara people."

"Are *you* Central African?" I ask.

"No, no," she says, "But Aji and Der'nube are."

I look at the cloth. "Can I touch it?" I ask.

"More than that," she says, "You're going to wear it."

I raise my eyes, sharply, "What?"

"I was raised in West Africa, part of a small pastoral tribe. I was about 6 when we were overrun by another tribe. I crawled into some weeds and hid while my people were massacred. When the attackers had left, I just started walking. Like you, in a way, everybody I'd had was gone. That's what I saw in your eyes. I saw the eyes of a refugee. I ended up at an international relief camp. I learned how to read and write there. I started preserving there. That's what I call it, collecting the echoes of people. Like Der'nube I kept bolts of fabric. I moved out of the camp eventually. I ended up going to medical school and then

116

immigrating and requalifying here. But I never stopped preserving. There are others like me, but most are Westerners. For them it is an academic exercise. For me... it is something more. I don't only preserve my own people though. There's so little I remember of them. I preserve others too."

She holds up the tablet, "This is a dictionary. When I hear about a tribe that has been destroyed, I search for dictionaries – those academics provide them. I go further, though. Language is important, but it is – more than most things – empty without those who speak it. My focus is art. Most of all, I collect fabric. I have a whole warehouse of fabric. This room is only a tiny sample of what I've collected."

She smiles, bittersweetly.

My eyes wander around the room. At all the fabrics gathered there. I've never seen anything quite like it.

"This is a museum of lost peoples," I say.

Dr. Abedi doesn't say anything.

She glances down at the cloth and says, "Do you know what Aji, means? In the Sara Kaba language?"

"No," I say, wondering why my team at the FBI had never asked this.

"It means 'salvation'."

"And Der'nube – do you know what that means?" she asks.

"No," I say.

"It means 'shield of G-d'."

"Why do they have those names?" I ask.

"I don't know. But when they left the Chosen, they were blank slates. I imagine they chose their own names. They see themselves as saviors and shields."

"Or it's all a con?"

"Very, very few people speak these languages. I had to look up the words on my tablet. This is a message they meant only for themselves."

"So what does it mean for me?" I ask.

Dr. Abade smiles.

"When I ran, I found another people. You have lost your people. They haven't simply disappeared though. They have turned on you. What you need is another people. Then, perhaps, you can survive."

I understand her. I'm not alone. I have Aji's people. I am thankful, once again, for this woman.

Over the coming hours, Dr. Abade uses putty to reshapes my eye sockets and jaw. She darkens my face and hands with makeup. She slings my arm with the fabric, but in a way that does not suggest an injury. Her movements are precise and careful. When she is done, I can barely recognize myself.

Finally, she dresses me in the weave of Der'nube's people.

I walk out into the street, restored and renewed.

I have no idea if I will survive.

I know, though, that I will never simply surrender.

Drop

Friday – 1:00 PM

My disguise is good enough to take the subway. Even so, I'm not willing to get off at the stop closest to Der'nube's hotel. Instead, I take it to Prospect Park, where all this seems to have started. The police I encounter look past me without a second glance. The disguise is excellent. I'm thankful that I ran into a sympathetic plastic surgeon.

As I start up the little street the hotel is on, I notice the surveillance. It isn't subtle. There are SUVs on the street, men on the roofs and 'pedestrians' milling around from place to place. I walk past them all, slowly and confidently. I'm sure they have my description. If I were to turn towards the hotel, they'd almost certainly pick me up. But walking past? Walking past I might just be able to do.

As I stroll by, I feel the eyes of the FBI and police all around me. I hope those of the fifth floor are as well. I take my time, both so that those in the hotel can see me *and* so that they have a chance to follow me. There's no point to any of this if they don't get my message.

A full two minutes after passing the hotel, I stop in front of the bodega. I'd seen the place on Google, at Dr. Abade's apartment. Even with the picture in front of us, we hadn't been able to decide where to leave the note. It needs to be found. Somehow, Aji's men need to know where to look. There's a stack of fruit and vegetables outside the store. I imagine there are cans and spices and milk inside. Nothing grabs my attention.

I don't have much time. My eyes scan the produce, looking for someplace only obvious to the right people. And then I see them, tangerines. The word is spelled out and it almost seems to echo Tangara. I grab a little paper bag. As I slip two of the fruit inside, I surreptitiously slide my note against the side of their little crate. Then I go inside, add a bottle of water to my little collection and pay.

When I step back out of the store, my peripheral vision picks up a young black man exiting the hotel parking lot. I recognize him as Aji's squad commander. I turn away from him and leave, hoping he'll be able to find what I've left him. The connection between tangerines and Tangara is a thin one. Maybe, though, he'll be able to draw it. When he does, he'll see my simple note: "Der'nube, meet me at the African Cultural Expo. Now. Dress appropriately."

I reach the end of the block without looking back. A few minutes later, I board a bus heading for Queens.

As the bus makes its frequent stops, I imagine what is happening all around me. Aji's followers, moving en masse to the subway. A fleet of surveillance personnel tracking and following them – trying desperately to be discrete in crowded and tight spaces. I imagine the entire hotel emptying, hundreds of people crowding out. I imagine them choosing different routes and different destinations.

The FBI can track a few people perfectly, but 150? That's not so simple.

An hour and two busses later, I'm at the entrance to the expo. Ahead of me is a world of confusion. People wearing clothing of every pattern and color weave and move through the enormous open space that makes up most of the exhibition. As I pay for my ticket, I smile. Tracking people in a place like this will be next to impossible. Not only that, but unless the FBI has a large store of African textiles on hand, it will be very hard for the surveillance to pass unobserved.

I pass through the gates, hoping I have a good lead on Der'nube. Even in this crowd, I want the best chance for privacy. I don't want to be seen. Somehow, SAC Miller will ensure that I don't survive if I am.

I'm barely through the entrance when I notice the Special Agents. Dressed in solid and bland colors, they stick out from all who surround them. I look at where they're looking and I see Der'nube, waiting patiently for me.

He must have taken a cab.

I walk right past him, as if he isn't there. But I know he isn't ignoring me. He can't help but see me, despite the riot of color and pattern, and despite my disguise. He can see me for the same reason you can hear your name called in a crowded room. I'm wearing his mother's pattern – it is a clear signal, even when surrounded by noise.

I walk slowly through the exhibition. I take in the smell of it; the chilis and the fried plantains and the dozens of other foods I can't even identify. I keep walking. I need to get Der'nube away from his surveillance and I have no idea how I'm going to do it.

I pass an exhibition of Igbo masquerade dancers, their incredible masked heads resting atop intricately costumed bodies as a heavy beat coordinates their movements. A crowd is watching them perform, but there is no place to hide. I continue, passing examples of nomadic huts constructed just for the expo. If I were to disappear into one of those, and Der'nube were to follow, I might never get out again. I keep walking.

I come to a booth selling textiles. I buy a large scarf, almost at random. Perhaps I'll throw it over Der'nube and conceal him.

I see him approaching out of the corner of my eye.

I stuff my purchase in a plastic bag and keep moving.

I'm running out of open space. The school building that houses the indoor parts of the expo looms ahead. It is one of those massive brick edifices first built during the Great Depression. Signs on the outside promise museum-quality exhibitions within. Knowing Der'nube is following, I keep walking. I push through the main doors. The stairs are blocked, everything is on the ground floor. Nonetheless, an array of options open to me. Galleries with southern African art, galleries of contemporary art. Galleries with pottery, masks, textiles and sculpture. I turn right, down the main hall. I flow through a mass of people. The doors on all the classrooms are open. As I look in each one, I just see traps; entrances without exits.

And then, up ahead I see my chance. An emergency exit. I keep walking, looking into the classrooms, checking that Der'nube is close behind. As I look into one classroom, I subtly gesture my head towards the emergency exit. I hope he notices, and his surveillance doesn't. He doesn't react, which is either good or bad.

Then I keep walking. I pass the last classroom and continue casually to the emergency exit. I come to the door and, as if by mistake, I push it open.

The fire alarm sounds. At that moment, Der'nube rushes forward and through the door. I step through right behind him. I whip the scarf I purchased out of my bag. Der'nube pushes the door closed and moments later I've tied the cloth into bowline knot around the exterior door handles.

I'm glad the FBI didn't only teach me how to shoot.

That done, the two of us dash from the door and disappear into the crowd. We slow down, but we both know we only have time for a brief conversation.

"Why did you want to talk?" asks Der'nube.

"I've been set up, Aji's been set up. We need your help," I say.

"How can I help?"

"You have a network. People working behind the scenes, right?"

"No." he says, simply.

"Come on," I say, "I know you have a network. You had a customs officer on speed dial."

"He was our case officer. We've kept in touch. Anyway, after the lies about the Department of Homeland Security why should I believe a word you say."

I don't have an answer for that. Then, suddenly, I do. "Der'nube, I swear on the soul of my brother that this is not a setup."

He looks at me. He sees my face. He nods and then he says, "Okay. But I still can't help. There is no secret network."

"There must be," I say, "Aji has an informant on *my* team in the FBI."

"Niesha, I swear, on the soul of my mother, that I have no idea who his contact is. If there is an informant, only Aji knows about it. The same goes for any sort of secret network."

I look up at him, in desperation. "I need to find people who can help me. Who can help Aji? Is there anything at all you can do?"

He closes his eyes for a moment, thinking.

Then he recites an address in Jackson Heights.

"What's there?" I ask.

"Our web manager, Alejandro Juarez. He has a list of all the people who have volunteered their services online. It's the best I can do."

And then, just like that, he turns away.

I walk briskly out of the expo. The FBI will be analyzing the video of Der'nube's escape from the ground floor of the school. My disguise has only got about 20 minutes of life left.

Information

Friday – 7:00 PM

I stop into a store near the expo and buy men's jeans, a very loose hoodie and a bit of make-up. At a busy bathroom in a transit center, I transform myself into a young African American man, my robe carefully folded into a plastic shopping bag. I adjust my makeup, adding highlights below my eyes to further confuse the facial recognition systems. Finally, I consciously modify my step – so that I walk male. The gait feels unnatural, but it further disguises who I really am.

Five minutes after walking into the restroom as an elegant African woman I walk out as a young black man in a hoodie. My broken arm rests within the hoodie's oversized pocket. It is better than nothing, but it still hurts. Despite my incredibly anonymous disguise, I try to hide my face from street cameras as I get on the subway and navigate my way to Roosevelt Avenue in Jackson Heights. At seven o'clock on a Friday evening, Jackson Heights is a crowded hive of activity. I grab dinner at a hole-in-the-wall Colombian joint – my hoodie close to my face in order to hide from the shop's cameras.

I turn up 86th Street and a few blocks later, the apartment buildings and stately houses near the main thoroughfare yield to modest freestanding homes lining a quiet and open street. Something seems eerily familiar about it; not in a good way.

As I walk, I start shaking involuntarily; just as I did when I arrested Aji. I think I know why. Up until now, I've been doing my best to hide. Now, I'm about to knock on the door of a stranger and introduce myself. The man will have every reason to turn on me as soon as I leave his house. The risk is total.

As I keep walking, I realize there's something more. It is when I come to a stop in front of the website manager's house that I realize what is really going on.

The houses on this street, in Jackson Heights, looks almost like the ones where LaMarcus was murdered on the South Side of Chicago. There is no nature strip between the road and the sidewalk, and the New York street feels a little more closed in – but the houses are unnaturally similar. There's something more, though. The web manager's house seems like an exact copy of the house LaMarcus was killed in front of.

When I lived on the South Side, I could ignore streets like this. They were just streets, streets I was going to escape from. But this place? I wasn't ready for this place. I wasn't ready to be reminded of the worst moment of my life.

My legs wobble underneath me. I grab onto the fence for support and just try to breath. I still have options. I can still turn around, hop on a train out of the city and, step by step, make my way as far from New York as possible. The odds of success as a fugitive are probably higher than the odds of overcoming SAC Miller and whatever cross-agency network he has at his disposal.

The fact is, the street is screaming warnings at me, just as another street had been when LaMarcus died. That time, I ignored the warnings. It seems reckless, at best, to do it again. I straighten up, deciding to run.

It is then that the pastor's words come back to me:

You gotta do what you can to raise people
up. Then you gotta rely on G-d for the rest.

Knocking on this door would be stupid. It isn't the same as it had been with LaMarcus, though. Walking home with LaMarcus, I'd ignored danger for no reason other than my own pride. Now? Now I'm ignoring it because I've gotta do what I can to raise people up.

Not only Aji, though. I've gotta raise up LaMarcus. I have to live for a purpose.

I breathe deeply.

Then I open the little gate and walk up the short path to the house. My heart is racing.

'I'm doing what I can,' I tell myself, 'I need to rely on G-d for the rest.'

I steady myself and then I knock on the door.

A few moments later, I hear a man's voice from behind the door. "Who is it?"

I don't know what to say. Do I just blurt out that I need his help? Do I give my name? Would either one lead to an open door? After a long pause I say, "Mr. Juarez, Der'nube sent me."

I hear the latch on the other side of the door move. Then, it opens.

The man holding the door is Hispanic and in his 50s. His face is weather-beaten, as if he'd worked for decades in the sun. Nonetheless, he is wearing a tailored shirt and expensive-looking glasses. Altogether, he gives off an air of extremely rugged sophistication. He'd do well in a commercial for some sophisticated but rough-edged alcohol.

"Who are you?" he asks.

"Can I come inside to tell you?"

"No." he says. The answer is flat and definitive.

"Okay," I say.

I don't know what else to do. I've got nowhere to go, not really. So I go all in. I pull my hood off and announce, "I'm Special Agent Neisha Jackson."

I see the emotions run over his face. Confusion. Recognition. Fear. Then, panic. He grabs me by my broken right arm and pulls me into his house. He's remarkably strong and the pain is overwhelming. I stumble in through the door, trying not to cry out.

Once inside, I manage to glance at my surroundings. The inside of the house isn't anything like what I'd been expecting. Sure, there's a little staircase that leads upstairs, there's a living room and there's a short hallway with a kitchen at the end. Every house on the street must have the same layout. But I am sure that not every house on the street has walls covered with massive murals in earthy tones of red and brown and gold. The murals themselves are lit up with museum-quality lighting. In the face of the overwhelming images and colors,

126

the house itself seems to fade into the background. The effect is mesmerizing.

I hear voices from the kitchen. A woman and a few children. We don't go there, though. Instead the man shoves me to the right and towards a door. He opens it and pushes me through.

We're in a small study. The parts of the walls not covered by bookcases or cupboards are, again, painted over with murals. A computer workstation sits in the corner.

The man roughly pushes me into a chair. He stands over me, dominating me. Then he asks, "Why are you here?"

"I want to help Aji," I say. I had thought this guy would wait until I was leaving to call the police. Now, I'm worried he's going to knock me out and call the police while we wait in his house.

"Yeah, I guessed that when the FBI announced you were wanted for murdering a witness." he says. In his case, it seems, being a friend of Aji's isn't enough of a reason for him to help me.

My mind scrambles for a better answer.

"Did you know the FBI has had it in for Aji?"

"Lady," he says, "I just manage the website."

I look him over. Alejandro Juarez is in his 50s, but he's powerfully built and seems like he's about to violently explode. He doesn't seem like a website manager.

"I was the lead investigator on his case. We were trying to pin something on him for over a year – like he was Al Capone. I had a whole team working on it."

"So?"

"Well, I thought we were investigating him because of a series of unexplained deaths. That was the reason *I* was investigating him. But I never found anything tying him to the murders. Until a few weeks ago. That was when we managed to draw a clear connection from Aji to the death of John Buckner."

"I saw that in the news conference, what about it?"

"Well, last night I decided to follow up. Instead of strengthening the case, though, I discovered it was all a setup."

"Yeah, what'd you find?" Alejandro's voice is disbelieving.

"The bartender they framed me for killing... He told me Aji was set up. Moments later, the man who was supposed to be guarding me burst through the door and shot and killed the bartender. He tried to kill me too."

Alejandro doesn't shift or speak. He is far from convinced.

"Can I move my arm?" I ask. I don't want to set him off.

He nods, watching me carefully.

I pull my hand from the pocket of my hoodie. It is empty. Then, using my other arm and moving gingerly with my still burnt hand, I pull the hoodie up and over my head. As I do so the man asks, "What the heck are you doing?"

The hoodie is off before I answer. Using my left arm, I point at my right, where Dr. Adabe had bandaged me.

"I was shot there."

"Show me?" he says.

"What?"

"Take the bandage off."

I don't really have a choice. I pull the bandage away from my skin. The little trench dug by the bullet begins to flow with blood.

Alejandro looks closely at the wound.

"Okay. You were shot. The news didn't say anything about that. Let's say you're telling the truth. Why the heck are you here?"

"Can I get a new bandage," I ask.

"Yeah," he says. He steps out of the room and returns with a first-aid kit. He asks, again, "Why are you here?"

"They intend to put Aji away forever. Or, kill him and kill me along the way. There's a powerful conspiracy which includes my boss at the FBI. I need to fight back."

"Lady, I'm just his web manager. I've got a family and a neighborhood that depends on me. I'll bandage you up, but beyond pretending you weren't here I'm not going to break the law for you — or for him."

"You've broken the law before, though, right?"

He stops wrapping and looks at me sharply.

"No." he says. He sounds deeply offended – almost like I'd assumed he was criminal because he's Hispanic and dresses in expensive clothes.

It is my turn to look doubtful. "You knew what a bullet wound looked like. Is that just from TV?"

"I had cousins who broke the law."

"Ah, and you're the world's strongest web manager because?"

"Because I was a landscaper for 30 years." The answer is flat and angry.

I suddenly feel deeply embarrassed. "Sorry, sorry for making assumptions."

He draws in a deep breath. "It's okay. I *was* trying to look like exactly the man you thought I was. You only drew the assumptions I wanted you to."

It is a surprisingly reasonable response. I'm not sure I would have given it, in his shoes. He finishes wrapping my arm and I pull my hoodie back on.

"How'd you go from a landscaper to a website manager?" I ask, hoping to build some kind of positive repartee. Our relationship seems to have turned a corner. The fierce monster of a man has been turned into something far more friendly.

"Oh, I'm more than a website manager. I run the IT department at a boutique Wall Street firm. I loved landscaping, but my body couldn't take it anymore – even just as a supervisor. I ran into Aji on the street. We got to talking. He said I spoke about landscaping the way some computer people he'd met spoke about what they did. Turns out he was right. That and I'm a darned good and experienced manager. I manage his website as a favor, that's all."

"Impressive," I say. And I mean it. Aji's only been in the US under three years. Pulling off that sort of career switch in that sort of time is pretty amazing.

I can see he's proud. Nonetheless, he says, "Ms. Jackson, you can butter me up, but I need you to get to the point and tell me why you're here."

"I need information, nothing illegal. Der'nube said you'd have a list of people who've registered on Aji's website and the services they've offered him. I need to find people, other people, who can help me."

"What kind of people are you looking for?"

"I don't know. I'll have to know it when I see it, I guess."

He thinks and then he goes to his desk, opens his laptop and logs in. "Should I just text you the list?"

"I don't have a phone," I say, shrugging. "I'm a fugitive, remember."

"Ah. Well, it's too long to print. So, come over here and take a look."

I hover behind him at the computer. He has a spreadsheet open.

"The list is simple," he says, "Name, address, phone, whatever they supplied. Then comments. That's where people offered things. There's one more column, which indicates whether we reached out to them. Not like mass mailings, but personally."

"Like if Der'nube asked for services."

"Right."

"How many entries do you have?"

"216,783."

"Wow."

"But we can filter it down."

A few clicks later, Alejandro says, "About 103,205 put comments in."

"Still a heck of a long list."

"Yeah."

"Let's start with those Aji's people contacted?"

"Only 467 of those."

We scan through the list quickly. Sound engineer. Stage builder. Social media coordinator. Bus driver. Composer. All the sorts of people who can help with a road show. And nothing the least bit helpful.

Just then, there's a knock at the door. A woman pokes her head in. I presume she's Alejandro's wife.

"What's going on in here?" she asks.

Alejandro gestures towards me with his head, "She's helping Aji. I'll get back to dinner soon."

The woman looks concerned, but she nods her assent and then backs out and closes the door.

"Let's get this done," says Alejandro.

"Okay," I say.

"Can you filter down on people who used words like 'can' 'make' or 'do'?"

A few clicks later the list is only 8,954 entries.

"Let's just start reading, okay?"

Alejandro starts scrolling through the list. People have offered a lot of different services. Some are just ads for things like communications services or website redesign. Others are lawyers or doctors. A few of the entries are sexual. Some offer violence. I ignore them all, I'm not going to seduce or overpower the FBI.

A few minutes pass and then I hear Alejandro take in a deep breath.

"What is it?" I ask.

He points at the screen, like he's afraid to say it. I read "If you need deepfakes, I can make them for you."

The address given is in Manhattan.

"What's a deepfake?" I ask.

"It's where you use AI, artificial intelligence, to create a video or a sound that looks like it came from somebody it didn't."

"Like impersonation?"

"Yeah, but a whole lot more convincing."

"Why would that be useful?"

"You're trying to get inside a conspiracy, right?"

"Right."

"Well, what could be better than pretending to be a member?"

"I could make a phone call and pretend to be somebody else?"

"I didn't tell you this, but, yeah."

"Wow."

Alejandro looks me over carefully. I can see him considering some kind of important decision.

I just wait.

Then, he stands up suddenly, moves some books from a bookshelf and opens a small safe. He pulls out two thick envelopes.

He hands me the envelopes. Inside are stacks of cash.

"It's $5,000. I keep cash so I can help people out when they're in trouble. I only make the kind of money I do because of Aji, so giving some to you kind of makes sense."

"Thank you," I say, genuinely grateful. Between transport, disguises and food my own resources had been growing thin.

Next, Alejandro reaches into his desk and grabs a USB drive. He plugs it in to his laptop. "I'm going to copy this list onto this drive. We also have a publicity network. People we send messages to about events and such. I'm going to put that on the drive too."

A few moments later, he hands me the little stick.

"I need to go back to dinner. Before I go, you need to know that if you get caught and they find out about me, I'll say you threatened my family. I don't have any other choice. Got it."

"Okay," I say.

The man shows me to the front door. I step outside. He closes it behind me, the world of his fantastic mosaics replaced with the mundane reality of his Jackson Height's street.

As I pass his little gate I look back at the house.

I hear the pastor's words in my head.

"You gotta do what you can to raise people up. Then you gotta rely on G-d for the rest."

I hope G-d remains reliable.

Deepfake

Friday – 9:00 PM

A row of buttons lines the wall of the foyer. Apartment numbers and a few names are written next to each one. I pick apartment 32, the one from the address, and hit the button. Nobody comes on the little speaker. Instead, a few seconds later, there's a buzz at the door and I'm admitted to the building.

I decide to take the stairs to the third floor. Getting trapped in an elevator, as unlikely as it might be, would be terrible. In under a minute and a half, despite the broken arm and bruises, I stop in front of apartment 32. I hit the doorbell.

Seconds later, a mousy woman in her early 20s is standing in front of me. She has brown hair and long, sloping, features. She's wearing a shirt that says, "I made a chemistry joke, but there was no reaction."

"Are you Lennon?" I ask.

She giggles. "Nope. I'm Emma. But come on in."

I step through the door. There's a small kitchen and common room there. The area is cluttered with cheap furniture and cheaper utensils. The surfaces reflect exactly the level of cleanliness you'd expect from graduate students living in shared accommodations. A short hallway extends in both directions with a series of doors leading off of it. I presume that they're bedrooms.

"Lennon!" Emma calls down one of the halls.

"Yeah?" comes a faint male voice.

"You got a visitor! A girl!" The last word is delivered teasingly.

A door in the hall opens. A young, disheveled, overweight white guy steps out briefly. He seems to be the stereotype of a programmer. He also seems to be wearing giant onesies pajamas.

"Whoa!" he says when he sees me. He pops back into his room. I hear furious sounds of movement and then he comes out again, dressed in jeans and another novelty T-shirt. This one has a picture of a skull with the words "Lather, Rinse, Repeat" beneath it.

I don't get it.

Lennon nervously walks towards the common room. He wipes his hand on his pants and extends it towards me. "Hi," he says, not quite making eye contact.

I shake his hand, a little reluctantly.

Emma giggles a bit. "Lennon, you gotta look girls in the eye."

I ignore the comment.

"Hi," I say, just like he did. Then figuring I probably have to take the lead I add, "I'm here on behalf of Aji Abakar."

At that, Lennon's face lights up. In his sudden excitement, he forgets his inhibitions and looks straight at me. "Seriously!"

"Yes," I say.

"Oh, man," he says, "I submitted that offer like a year ago. That's so cool!"

Emma looks curious.

"What offer?" she asks.

"You know what I'm working on, right?" he asks. It is a half-question for me, half-statement aimed at Emma.

I have no idea why I'd know what he's working on.

"Nope," I say, as pleasantly as I can manage.

"Oh, man," he says, "There was a whole lot of press about it like 6 months ago. They called it 'the Altruistic AI'."

Emma snorts. "For complete disclosure, the headline in the New York Reporter was 'Our New Artificially Intelligent, but Altruistic, Overlords."

Lennon glowers at her. "Yeah, well, you don't know why I got into it, do you?"

Emma shrugs. I just watch.

"It's this guy, Aji. I saw a YouTube clip about him. He was talking about blessing. He said when you bless somebody, you create *opportunities* for them. And I thought, dude, I can make deepfakes, maybe he can use that to bless somebody. So, I submitted something on his website. Then I just forgot about it. Well, the Aji part anyway. But the whole idea of blessing people? That stuck with me. When I saw that video, I was working on a pretty cool problem for my doctorate. There's this moral and legal problem with self-driving cars. It is pretty basic: do you prioritize the passengers lives over other peoples'?"

He looks at me, expectantly.

"Uh, I don't know," I say, guessing he meant to ask me a question.

"Exactly! Are two people in the car worth more than 2 outside? No matter what the choice, the car company can be sued into oblivion and the engineer who helped design it will live with the horror of his decisions on his mind. Right."

"Right." I say.

"Well, I had a cool idea. I decided to use another form of AI to go *around* the problem. We were building an AI that would look at accident records and compare them against social media posts, job titles, home addresses, car types and lots of other public data. Using this data, the AI model can determine the moral choices the driver would make – based on drivers like him or her who had to make similar decisions in the past. So, even though the car's owner isn't driving a self-driving car, *their* morality would still be steering it, so to speak. We'd cut the car company and the engineers right out of the moral loop. Really, we were seeing how closely we could model the most human of decisions through AI."

"That sounds pretty cool," I say, genuinely impressed.

"Yeah, well, then I watched Aji's video. I was doing some seriously cutting-edge AI work, but I didn't know how that could help him. So, I decided to offer some deepfake work. I'd just use off-the-shelf software for it – although I'd tweaked it some. Nobody ever got back to me though and his whole idea of blessing was just sitting there, demanding that I think about it."

Lennon's voice is picking up speed.

"I thought, you know, I'm not doing enough *blessing* with this car thing. I want to really empower people, not just imitate them. So, I asked my advisor if I could switch projects. The new project was even more ambitious. I wanted an AI that could bless people. Cool, huh?"

"How can an AI bless people?" I asked.

"First, I had to train the AI to recognize empowerment. That's blessing, right? Normally philosopher types take the easy way out. They go with utilitarianism: the most happiness for the most people. Then, to make it actually measurable, they use money as a stand in for happiness. They end up looking at incomes to determine utility to determine what provides the most good for the most people. There are *all sorts* of problems with every one of those steps, but philosophers are not very good at dealing with reality. The cool thing is, an AI doesn't need to think that way. It doesn't have to *measure* things; it just has to recognize patterns. So, we could ask, what is the pattern of empowerment – or its opposite? We looked at economic mobility, children's education and earnings, crime rates, drug use, mental health, divorce rates, quality of life, book sales, savings and so on. We even correlated survey data on happiness, hopefulness and such with demographic data from those same surveys. The system learned to look at all of this stuff and make a sort of biography for a subject and then ask a simple question: was the subject being looked at more or less empowered than before? Not just financially but socially, mentally and so on. There are actually lots of simultaneous scales. And we validated and calibrated the whole thing with human reviews and surveys of actual people we'd assessed."

Lennon's eyes are glowing with excitement.

"Here comes the AI overlord bit," says Emma.

Lennon grins, "Yeah. Because then we connected *government policy* to those shifts in empowerment. The AI, and we're still working on it, is being trained to recognize when policies bless people, and when they don't. It is like a Congressional Budget Office but for personal achievement. It is seriously hardcore stuff. We're really pushing the boundaries of AI, but we're all learning a lot from it. The system has already spit out some pretty cool ideas. There's a long way to go though. I mean, take me. I've been empowered because I watched a five-minute video of Aji. He doesn't even know me. You can't measure that. Even so, if this AI works, Aji could be blessing entire societies because of that video. I mean, that's cool, isn't it?"

"Uh, yeah," I say. I mean it, but I'm still trying to track everything he's said.

"While we work on the AI," Lennon adds, "That whole blessing thing has become like my moral guide. Before I make a decision, I ask which choice will empower people more. And that's the choice I make. Well, most of the time – I still get greedy. It is a really cool way to think. But up until now, I didn't even know if Aji got my submission. Now you're here! I'm probably boring you. A lot of people say I bore them. So, what does Aji want?"

Lennon looks like an excitable puppy.

"Well, this is going to be a doozy of a question for your moral calculator."

"What is?" asks Lennon, excited.

Emma looks a bit worried.

"Did you know Aji was arrested?" I ask.

Lennon looks at me, incredulous. "What? What for?"

"Murder," I say.

"Whoa!" says Lennon, "I didn't see that coming."

"Oh, he didn't do it," I say.

"Yeah, you'd say that" says Emma, with a bit of a sneer.

"Do you know who I am?" I ask her, hoping I'm not walking myself into serious trouble by bringing yet another person in on my identity.

"I'm guessing you're like some kind of errand girl for Aji," she says.

"Not quite," I say, "I'm the FBI Special Agent who built the case against him and arrested him."

"Whoa!" says Lennon.

Emma looks sideways at him, "*I* didn't see that coming."

I can't help but smile.

"Now I really wanna know why you're here," says Lennon.

"Last night I was talking with a witness and I realized that my boss set Aji up. I worked out how he did it. I worked out how he fed me the evidence. I was just putting it all together when somebody else who was in on *his* conspiracy came in, shot my only witness and tried to kill me too. Now, I'm a fugitive accused of murder. You can read the news and find out all about it. I want you to help Aji and I want you to help me too."

They just stare at me. It is their turn to try to catch up. Then after a few seconds, Lennon puts it together. He smiles, "You want the deepfakes to penetrate their conspiracy."

He's pretty bright.

"Yeah," I say.

"To do what?" asks Emma.

"Aji isn't guilty. At least not of this crime. But the conspiracy against him is willing to kill those who know about it. I want to break him out of prison before he disappears forever. Once he's out, we can use *his* network to deal with the conspiracy."

"Whoa," says Lennon.

Emma smirks.

Lennon closes his eyes. He starts rapidly muttering to himself, like he's doing calculations in his head. Then he flashes his eyes open, looks me straight in the eyes and says, "I'll do it."

Emma asks, "Why?"

"If I can help Aji establish his innocence, then lots of people will be blessed. If he isn't innocent, then he'll be tracked down and the criminal justice system will be reinforced. It's a win-win – so long as *we* don't get caught."

He seems to be winking at her.

Emma bites her lower lip, thinking. Then she smiles and says, "Well, okay, I can help with that."

A few minutes later, I've handed over the USB chip, and laid out the basics of my idea. With that, the three of us start in on the hard work of making it actually happen.

Setup

Saturday – 1:30 PM

We listen as the phone rings. A moment later a pre-recorded voice asks, "FBI New York Field Office. If you know your party's extension, please enter it now. Otherwise..."

I enter SAC Miller's extension. He's almost certainly at work, even on a Saturday afternoon. If he isn't, his extension will ring through to his cell.

It seems odd, calling SAC Miller. It seems even odder considering our surroundings. When I'd thought of the work of a hacker, I'd always imagined people chugging Mountain Dews and Red Bulls in darkened basements. But Emma, Lennon and I are sitting in a café just a few blocks north of Foley Square. We're enjoying lattes served up by a smiling and friendly barista. And we're breaking more laws than I can count.

We had been up all night, working to set this into motion. It wasn't a simple operation. Luckily for me, Emma's chemistry T-shirt was her boyfriend's. She's actually getting a Ph.D. in cybersecurity. She'd spent the entire night setting up the relays that would hide our tracks and scramble the FBI's response. Star Wars jokes aside, and there were a few, I got the impression that the good guys in cybersecurity were never far from the dark side. That done, Lennon set up the deepfake itself. He downloaded hours upon hours of recordings of our target and used them to train an AI to speak just like the target. The fact that we'd be doing this over the phone helped, it cut out lots of frequencies the AI wouldn't have to master. It also meant the system could just learn what it needed to in the little time we had.

Finally, I fine-tuned the plan as the two of them taught me about the powers, and limits, of their hacking and deepfake capabilities.

Now, we're here, sipping Lattes with headphones plugged into a single laptop I purchased with Alejandro's cash in Midtown. Picking the laptop was easy. As I'm a fugitive who might not know when I'll have a chance to plug in, we bought the computer with the longest battery life.

While the deepfake was being trained to speak like the target, we pre-loaded a list of expected phrases that I could activate with a touch. But the unexpected could happen. To deal with this, Lennon set up a system that will recognize *my* words and then speak them in the target's voice – almost instantaneously. It wasn't perfect, the delay would seem a little unnatural, but we had to make do with what was possible. What we were doing, even with the considerable computing resources Lennon had at his disposal, was not exactly easy.

Initially, I'd wanted to have a few voices to work with. We couldn't do that though. The AI needs a library of recordings from the subject. At one extreme, the deepfake target couldn't possibly be Marshall Johnson – not unless we tapped his phone. At the other extreme, it could easily be the President of the United States. The only problem with that was that the possibility of her calling SAC Miller was low.

Thankfully, there was a useful target right in the middle: Sheila Markoff, the politically cut-throat Director of the FBI.

After a few rings, SAC Miller picks up the phone. "Director?" he says. Emma's relays have successfully managed to spoof the caller ID. Apparently, that isn't as hard as it should be.

"Good morning, Miller," says the voice of Director Markoff, after I tap the prompt on the screen.

"What's going on?" asks Miller.

Another tap, "You need to move Aji to the MCC."

The MCC is the Metropolitan Correctional Center, a detention facility a few blocks from the FBI offices. It has housed some of the most dangerous prisoners in Federal History, including terrorists, drug lords and mobsters.

None have ever escaped.

"Why?" asks Miller.

Another tap, "We've gotten some recent chatter on channels related to Aji's organization. They're planning something big for *this afternoon.* I think Neisha is going to try and break Aji out of the FBI offices. We need to move Aji, quickly, to someplace more secure."

There *has* been chatter. We'd generated it. We'd broken Aji's publicity list into three parts. The FBI identities, which I recognized, were bundled with a host of less involved Aji supporters. I recorded a message for them, telling them both Aji and I were innocent and asking them to gather at Battery Park at 1:45PM for a 20-minute protest march up to Foley Square. I asked them, if possible, to wear African robes in solidarity.

Thousands of people have already shown up at Foley Square. If I were Miller, it could certainly look like cover for something audacious.

Miller says, "Come on, Sheila –"

I suddenly panic. First names? Does Director Markoff call Miller James or Jim? I write out a quick note on a notepad, asking Lennon to change all the 'Miller's to 'Jim's. I hope I got it right.

Miller is still speaking, "Given what you really know about her, do you really think Neisha suddenly going to try to break into the Federal Building?"

The suggestion of my innocence in that sentence gives me chills. Is the Director part of the conspiracy?

That's not good.

Thankfully, it was one of the possibilities we'd mapped out.

"Jim," Director Markoff's voice says calmly, "We've pushed her to the wall. We don't know what she'll do. Remember, Aji has a mole in your office so she might just be able to pull it off."

I hear SAC Miller sigh. At least he doesn't seem to have responded badly to the Jim. I *guess* we got it right.

"Okay. I'll get it done."

Another tap. "When?"

"Well, it sounds like the marchers will be here in about 45 minutes. I've got to get things ready here. Maybe 30 minutes?"

"Okay, one more thing," says the Director's voice, "Don't use Foley Square. We believe they're planning on gathering there."

"Got it," says SAC Miller.

A moment later, the line goes dead.

Just in case Miller decides to check whether the *real* Markoff has called him, Emma has rerouted the Director's cell and office phone. If he places a call to the Director, it'll go straight to us.

"Whoa," says Lennon, "That sounded an awful lot like the Director of the FBI is in on this conspiracy you've been talking about. That, and the conspiracy actually exists."

I ask, "Any response to the other messages?"

The *other* messages were to a stronger group of Aji supporters. People we *hoped* would be willing to break the law. They were sent only to those with secure messaging apps. The other messages didn't tell people to gather at the hotel. They told them to keep a low profile and to come directly to the area surrounding Foley Park.

They'd get further instructions when they got there.

"Yeah," says Lennon, "About 500 people agreed to show up."

I smile. No matter what 'Director Markoff' claimed, I couldn't break Aji out of the FBI offices. The FBI, though, could.

I finish my coffee, pack up my laptop and stand up to leave.

"Thanks," I say, "For everything."

The two of them nod and I walk out of the café.

If the plan goes as well as I hope it will, I'll go from being 'just' a wanted fugitive to being public enemy number one. Once Aji is out, Emma and Lennon will do everything they can to burn any trace of what they have done.

As interesting and as impressive as their work has been, I doubt I'll ever see either one of them again.

Freedom

Saturday – 1:50 PM

I walk the few blocks down to the corner of Duane Street and Broadway. I'm standing directly across the street from the Jacob Javits Federal Building and I feel *incredibly* exposed. The FBI is looking for me and, at this very moment, SAC Miller could literally look his window and see me, standing here, waiting.

It can't be helped though; this is where I need to be.

I'm dressed in a raincoat wrapped tightly around Dr. Abedi's African robes. Nothing suspicious there, right? I'm not terribly worried about being picked up on camera. It turns out hackers and AI specialists know even more than I do about fooling facial recognition systems. Lennon and Emma not only worked on my appearance, they tested their work on a facial recognition system they had set up in their apartment. People aren't AI's though. What fools a computer won't necessarily fool a person.

I glance across the street at the cop sitting in a hardened post next to a row of bollards protecting the FBI's side of Duane Street. I nod at him and he nods back. I'm try very hard to look like I'm waiting for somebody. I hope he doesn't pay me too much attention.

Ten minutes later, a man walks up to me. He's young and black. He's carrying a Walgreen's bag. I lean forward and greet him like I've known him for years. I even give him a little kiss on the cheek. Then, hand in hand, we begin to walk slowly, very slowly down the block. I slip my laptop into the plastic bag and then take the bag itself from the man. I don't have two working arms; I can't carry two things. Out of the corner of my eye I see a large, armored, van pull to the bollards. The cop in the little bulletproof hut hits a button and the bollards lower.

I don't have a phone because I'm trying to keep myself under the radar. I can imagine exactly what's happening, though. We'd picked one of the highly motivated Aji supporters at random. We'd asked him to text Emma and Lennon when a potential prisoner transport van exited the parking lot. We couldn't work out a way of *knowing* whether any particular van has Aji in it. So, we had to ask. When they got the text, Emma and Lennon would use the deepfake again to call SAC Miller and check on the status of the transfer.

If the first possible prisoner van is *our* van, then SAC Miller will confirm it – happily informing the Director of the FBI that the van has just left the building. If not, then we'll go with the next van – and take our chances that there aren't too many prisoners being moved on a Saturday afternoon.

Thankfully, SAC Miller told the "deepfake Director" that this was the van. I know this for a simple reason: As the van pulls past the bollards, a crowd seems to emerge like a fog from the side streets. It is particularly dense at Reade Street, one block down.

I know that text messages are being sent to each of the 500 people here. Like chess pieces they are being told to converge on the block. A few hundred will block the van at Reade Street and a few hundred more will come up behind the van and block its retreat near Duane Street. At any normal part of Broadway, the van might be able to drive up on the sidewalk or take advantage of the road's width to find a weak spot in the crowd. This, however, is not a normal part of Broadway. Heavy concrete barriers have been placed specifically to block off the lanes on the side closest to the Federal buildings that line the road. Additional concrete dividers protect the opposite sidewalk. In the interests of stopping car bombs and vehicular attacks, the normally three-lane Broadway has been reduced to only two lanes with concrete barriers preventing any vehicle from deviating from this narrow path. 500 people can block two lanes of traffic.

The van pulls onto Broadway. As it proceeds lazily down the street, the crowd suddenly surges in front of it. The driver can see what's happening. He pulls to a screeching halt and slams the vehicle into reverse. He's too late though. Hundreds more people are jumping the concrete barriers and crowding the road at the intersection of Duane and Broadway. The driver might be willing to run down a few people to deliver his prisoner. Killing dozens is another matter, entirely.

Within 30 seconds of turning onto Broadway the van is trapped.

The cop in the booth is already calling in reinforcements. I can see him do it. The Federal Building has a special contingent of police and hundreds of other officers can be mustered pretty quickly. We need to move fast.

We are moving fast.

Just as the van was identified, text messages were sent to the marchers coming up from Battery Park. Thousands more protestors will be joining the 500 hard-core supporters who have trapped the van. Press coverage will come with them.

The hope is that a hard and sharp operation against peaceful religious protestors would look very bad indeed.

On cue, the crowd surrounding the van begins to shout: "FREE AJI! FREE AJI!"

I maneuver near the rear door of the vehicle.

Less than two minutes later, the dedicated force at the Federal Building rushes out and takes positions north of us. I also see the first of the African-robed protestors join the crowd around the van. Less than a minute later a dozen cops have arrayed themselves a few hundred feet from the crowd in preparation for *something*. Of course, in the same brief time period, we've gone from 500 people to more than 2,000.

Our advantage won't last long. We have maybe 15 minutes before hundreds more police show up. They'll form riot-control lines and, with tear gas support, begin to move through the crowd. One way or another they *will* disperse the crowd and they will arrest a fair number of people along the way. The concrete barriers will work against us and everything we've done will have achieved nothing.

That isn't really the deadline though. In perhaps five minutes, the police will have a large enough cordon to stop anybody they want – myself and Aji included – from leaving the scene.

Realistically, we have fewer than five minutes to get Aji out of the van and on the move.

"FREE AJI! FREE AJI!"

The crowd is growing in size and volume. I can imagine the press filing their first reports. I can imagine notifications reaching SAC Miller, Director Markoff and the rest of the conspiracy. I can imagine SAC Miller looking out his window and seeing us gathered here.

I can only hope the rest of the plan is coming together. Director Markoff must be trying to call SAC Miller. Emma couldn't do some precise rerouting of her attempts to reach the Special Agent in Charge. The protections around her communications were too extensive. Instead, she messed with *everything* on the local side of the FBI communications. Any call to the FBI in New York from outside of New York will reach some random extension. She'd have to get very lucky to actually contact Miller. The real Director Markoff could *email* SAC Miller. We can only hope that she wouldn't do that in an emergency – at least not quickly.

The "deepfake Director" has no such issues. Right now, I hope, SAC Miller's phone is ringing. Our deepfake of Director Markoff is on the other end of the line. She's explaining to "Jim" that she's afraid this is going to be another Waco. That we need to let Aji out of the van before the FBI takes a major public-relations hit.

Given that I'm still waiting, I'm guessing he's not going for it. He wants to wait for the riot police. I can appreciate his argument: time is on his side. More cops seem to be showing up by the second.

I hope the 'Director' is patiently explaining that in China the government gives protestors everything they want – and then arrests them a few weeks or months later. Once the heat has died down. I'm hoping she's arguing that nobody denies the power of *that* state.

But it seems that SAC Miller is not convinced.

A policeman points at me. They've recognized who I am. A small contingent begins to push its way through the crowd, towards me.

The clock is running out far faster than I'd imagined it would.

I hope our last resort works. I hope the 'Director' is ordering SAC Miller to let Aji out. I hope, in the world of the conspiracy, that *he's* not the one in charge.

I hope it works because if it doesn't, things will get very bad very quickly.

The cops are 20 feet away, trying to push through the crowd. It is then that the back door of the van opens. I glance inside. My heart jumps when I see Aji standing there, his shackles off. I'm shocked by the strength of my reaction. Aji is wearing an orange jumpsuit, designed specifically to make it hard to disappear. I don't see Johnson. I would have thought he'd be assigned to this prisoner transport. Maybe he's on sick leave due to the hit he took.

Aji strides towards the door and then steps to the threshold of the van. The crowd erupts in cheers.

"Get down here!" I say, urgently. He steps down from the van. I put the Walgreen's bag on the pavement and with my one good arm I pull out an orange-dominated Agbaba (a West African robe). I hand it to him. He slips it over his head. The overwhelming color of the jumpsuit fades away behind the bold patterns of the African fabric.

In that instant, he is made almost indistinguishable from the rest of the crowd.

I pick up the bag (which still has my computer) and start running from the police. Aji follows. We race through the crowd. It clears for us, just a bit. It doesn't seem to have cleared for the police though, and we quickly put distance between us. Then I kneel once more, put down the bag and take off my raincoat with my one good hand. I stuff it into the bag. By the time I stand up again, I am just another dot in a crowd full of color.

Then the final planned text message comes: "Disperse!"

I know it does because moments later, the crowd heads off in every direction. Robed, plain-clothed, black, white and just plain numerous. They jump the barriers. They push past the outnumbered police. We join them, two people in an untraceable mass. Just in case, Emma was going to try her hand at messing with the video surveillance in the area.

Five minutes later, we've left the scene far behind.

I can only imagine what we've left behind: an empty van on an empty street and both a legitimate organization and an illegal conspiracy trying to piece together what happened. I can imagine the accusations that are beginning to fly.

We've done it though. I've got Aji.

Finally, I can rely on *his* network. *His* contacts. *His* people. I won't need to keep pulling miracles from inside an invisible hat.

I've got Aji! I feel almost giddy with the realization.

When we reach the corner of Canal and Lafayette, a few blocks from the scene, Aji turns to me.

His eyes are dark with anger.

His voice barely more than whisper, he says, "You really shouldn't have done that."

I'd expected gratitude. Maybe even a touch of awe. But anger?

I can't even begin to understand why Aji Abakar would be angry.

Resistance

Saturday – 2:30 PM

"What?" I ask, too shocked, disappointed and *angry* to form a more complex thought.

Aji continues, "After everything you've learned you haven't worked it out? I'm a *curse*. People who curse me are cursed. Now, they can watch video of me breaking out of jail?!? They can see me defying the rules and attacking the justice system. Who is going to bless me for that? Only the people who *already* liked me. But the rest? They'll curse and they'll be cursed. *How could you do that?*"

"You being locked up; it wasn't *justice*." I say.

"What wasn't justice? That a man who's killed more people than you've known ends up in jail? That a man who continues to be responsible for suffering, suffers?"

"You didn't kill John Buckner."

"So what? Somebody did. *And they did it because of me.* How does breaking me out of jail help with that?"

"I thought you said you wanted an angel of justice."

"I want an angel of justice. That doesn't mean somebody who comes to my defense."

"Maybe it does. *Somebody* decided to set you up for the murder of John Buckner. Don't we have to deal with *them*? Don't *they* need justice?"

"They've cursed me. G-d will take care of them."

For a moment, I'm flabbergasted. Then I shoot back, "So, you just want to stand back and do nothing and hope G-d balances the scales."

"Balances the scales? I said whoever set me up cursed *me* and will be cursed. I didn't say they would *deserve* to be cursed. There's no balancing that I can understand."

I want to shout, but it would attract too much attention.

"Listen, Aji, I'm simple. I don't work in crazy riddles like that. I can deal with one thing at a time. You didn't kill John Buckner, so I needed to set you free."

"You're simple? Rallying thousands of people to break me out of a police van at just the right time and place is simple? If you have your evidence, present it and get the charges pulled. *That's simple*. And nobody would curse me for it. Everybody wins."

"That's what I *wanted* to do. Except my boss is the one who set you up."

"So, go to the press. Make your case there."

"Then he had my bodyguard charge in and shoot the only witness who knew about it. He meant to kill me too. I escaped so he did the next best thing he could and set *me* up for the murder. My boss went on TV and everything."

Aji's anger seems to fall away. "They killed Mike?" he says.

"The bartender? I think that was his name, yeah."

"Fuck."

I've never heard Aji swear.

"Mike was a good guy. A very good guy. If you really want justice, shove me in front of a truck and end this." he says.

"Aji, *you* didn't kill him. *They* killed him. *They* ordered it. *They* pulled the trigger. *We* need justice."

"Oh, and how are you going to get it?"

"That's the other reason I broke you out."

"What are you talking about? How does breaking me out help?"

"Aji, I can't deal with this alone. I've done everything I can. But I need your network."

"My network?"

"Yeah. The way I figured it, *your* conspiracy might just trump theirs."

He snorts. "Neisha, I don't have a conspiracy."

"Aji, stop playing games on this. You had an informant on my team. Inside the FBI. You got ahold of my college essay. You have incredible people in incredible places."

"I never said I had a conspiracy."

"So how in the heck did you get my college essay?"

"Somebody in your office messaged me the night you found the so-called evidence against me. They didn't give their name; the account was anonymous. But they talked about you. They said you'd spent a year chasing phantom leads in an effort to make a random pattern into a crime. They said that wasn't why they joined the FBI. So, *they* got ahold of your file, read it, and became convinced you were on some sort of unholy vendetta. The message said you were a fanatic. They had proof. The proof was your college essay. That's it. That's my mole in the FBI."

"One anonymous message?" I ask.

"A long message, but just one message."

The window of hope seems to shrink in front of me. I won't let it close though. "Maybe you got other messages from other people. Maybe we can reach out to them. Maybe we can *create* a conspiracy."

He just shakes his head, "Neisha, I don't even know who this person was. There is no conspiracy, and I can't build one. More importantly, I won't."

"What do we do then?"

He doesn't reply. Not at first.

Then he says, "You shouldn't have broken me out."

"I had to," I say, "You're innocent and they never would have let you go." I don't add that I *wanted* to rescue him; and that I desperately wanted his gratitude.

He doesn't answer. He doesn't need to. I know what he wants to say. As we keep walking, no destination in mind, I look around and notice a remarkable thing. More and more people seem to be coming out into the streets dressed in African clothes. Women, children, whites, blacks, Hispanics and even Asians.

All of them trying to stand with Aji.

As we pass one old white woman in an ill-suited African dress, I turn to Aji and say, "They are dressing up in solidarity with you."

"They will be blessed," he says. But there is no warmth in it. No appreciation. For him, it is just a statement of fact.

We just keep walking.

We are in midtown when I hear footsteps rushing up behind me. I feel a brief jolt of fear. Just as quickly, it melts away. I suddenly don't care. Hopelessness has become acceptance, as if I have reached the end of a process of mourning.

I don't run. I don't prepare to fight. When I feel a tap on my shoulders, I begin to lift my hands to my head.

"No, no," says the voice behind me in some sort of Indian accent.

I turn around. There's no Special Agent there. No policeman. No Marshall. There's just a middle-aged hotdog vendor. In his hands are two hotdogs with all the fixings.

He says, "You forgot your food."

He thrusts the hotdogs towards us.

"We didn't buy hotdogs," I say.

He just smiles, winks, and says, "Free Aji."

Aji reaches forward and takes his hotdog. I do the same.

Then the hotdog vendor turns and walks back to his cart.

The man has committed a crime: aiding fugitives from justice. And for what? Is there any point to any of it? We keep walking, but I still don't know where we're going or what we're trying to achieve.

At around 75th and Madison, Aji says, "Der'nube told you about the Prophet, right?"

"Yes." I say, "He was the leader of the Chosen."

"When I was in the jungle, I thought he was more than that. I thought he was a Prophet of G-d."

"How could you, when you saw what he was doing?"

"Have you read the Book of Numbers? The killings, the genocides? The ideas are there. Not that that proved anything to me. I didn't know anything about the Bible before he chose me. What I did know, what we all knew, was that the Prophet was always victorious. If he claimed G-d delivered his victories, how could I argue? For us, the rest was just window dressing."

He laughs bitterly. "We really seemed to be building a chosen people, too. We were blessed with victory in our holy endeavor... but I loathed every moment of it. Neisha, I killed my own parents so that I could survive. It doesn't matter that the Chosen told me to. *I* did it.

152

Then I took the lives of so many others – so *I* could survive. I hated myself as much as I hated G-d and His Prophet."

I turn towards him. The pain on his face is obvious.

"It wasn't your fault, Aji. You didn't have a choice. If you hadn't lived, some other child would have taken your place. Nobody would have had their lives spared."

"Neisha, you can see the *mathematics* of it. You're far from it. You can count lives. But I *lived* it. Yes, if I hadn't chosen to kill then my victims still would have died. But *I* wouldn't have been the one killing them."

I remember the other child soldiers talking about the *way* he killed. The way those who died were uplifted by him. "Aji, others slaughtered but you tried to end lives with honor and dignity."

"Is that what you heard from Der'nube and the others?"

"Yes."

"They didn't understand, then. They never understood. I wasn't trying to make those I killed feel better. They *were* better. Every time I took a life, I was just learning how much better. They were better because they died and would never become killers. Their deaths showed their greatness, in and of themselves. My soul, though, was corrupted the first time I pulled that trigger. If I had been better, I would have died with my parents. Instead, each time I took a life I kept telling myself I'd eventually find some kind of salvation."

"So why did you do all the killing for your squad. Why not let them do their share?"

"Neisha, that was one of my justifications. I was trying to protect *their* souls from *my* horror."

A question strikes me, "What kind of salvation were you hoping for?"

"One that almost came," he says with a grimace, "Der'nube told you about the Prophet summoning me?"

"Yes," I say.

"Well, even Der'nube doesn't know the whole story. The Prophet thought he was going to kill me. His men thought he was going to kill me. But I was the one who was going to kill him. I believed he was a prophet of Almighty G-d and I was going to kill him anyway. Can you imagine that?"

I try, but I can't. I can't imagine any of it. I just shake my head.

"That was the last time I held a gun. The Chosen didn't have pistols. Only the Prophet did. He was afraid of us, really. The lack of pistols was a way he kept himself safe. It is hard to hide an AK-47 on the body of a 12-year-old. But I'd found a pipe which was the perfect size. The body of an AK cartridge fit in the pipe, but the rim didn't – just like on my rifle. When I came to the Prophet, I held that loaded pipe in one hand. In the other, I had the firing pin. I'd practiced slamming one against the other, again and again until I knew I could do it perfectly. When they brought me to the Prophet, they didn't search me. I wouldn't be close enough to use a knife and I couldn't possibly have had a gun. Instead, they shoved me to my knees a safe distance in front of him.

"I was going to kill him. Then I was going to die. But I didn't do it right away. I held back. Maybe, I didn't want to die. I *know* I didn't want to die. *That* time, when my own life was at risk, I didn't kill. That time, he looked in my eyes and a moment later, I'd lost my chance."

"He died though."

"Yes, but *I* didn't take him. *I* didn't act. Instead I got that prophecy. His only *real* prophecy: "Those who bless you will be blessed and those who curse will be cursed." I didn't believe any of it. All I knew is that I'd missed my chance. My squad rescued me. As I'm sure they told you, the first village we came to was cursed but the second was blessed. When I saw that, I thought I could be redeemed. Not in some small African village, though. It wasn't big enough. I thought maybe I could come here and I could spread blessing all over the world. I could make *something* right. But that was the worst decision of all."

He stops and takes in a long and ragged breath. "I didn't know my curses has led to hundreds being wounded and over 30 people being killed. *You* told me that. I'd only known about 4 people. When you told me about 30, I couldn't help but ask myself: 'Who didn't she discover?' I kept wondering how much deeper I'd dug my own hole.

In Garubia it was life or death. If I didn't kill, I would have died. But I didn't have to come here. I could have stayed in that village. And now you've broken me out the curses will spread."

We've almost reached 110th Street, but I still don't know where we're going.

I can't help but ask, "What happened to the confident, wise, man in the interrogation room? To the man on the weekly broadcasts? To the one who seems to have all the answers?"

"Special Agent Jackson, it was all an act. A desperate attempt to bless and empower and enable. I can't quite explain it, but I even wanted to protect and enable and empower you – the fanatic bent on destroying me. I didn't want you to go after me because you would have been cursed. The very idea pained me. When I had my chance, I made up a different interpretation of that college essay. I even convinced you of it. Not because I wanted you to rescue me. But because I wanted *you* to be blessed."

I'm stunned by that. "You convinced me I was chosen. You convinced me I'd put my life on the line in the service of justice. How could you not have believed it?"

"Neisha, look at where we are and what we're doing. Whether or not I *was* right about you, I *am* now."

As I think about that, I realize it's true. Whether it was some sort of elaborate bluff or not, Aji tests and interpretations have defined me.

Aji continues, "I lift up others just because I'm desperate to escape what I have done."

I imagine he'd lift up others even without that reality. Maybe, though, he's in the middle of his own test.

"Did you drink to destroy yourself?" I ask. I can imagine Aji in that bar, spilling out his soul to Mike – the only man who knew his pain. I ache with the sadness of that image.

"No," says Aji, "I can't destroy myself. People can't see my weakness. Even before the curse they couldn't see my weakness. In the jungle, with the Chosen, I took the drugs. I just didn't let the others see me do it. I had to let them think there was a better way, despite the fact that I wasn't strong enough to take it. No, I drink for the same reason I took the drugs. To dull my reality."

Escaping reality was the last thing I'd expected from this man.

"If you need everybody to think you're strong, then why show *me* you're weak?"

Aji waits a long while before he answers. "Do you know what a Sonderkommando was?"

"No?" I say.

"A Sonderkommando was a Jew who was forced to help operate the gas chambers during the Holocaust. A Sonderkommando would lead untold thousands of people to their deaths. He couldn't tell them a thing. He was complicit in every part of the process. If he didn't perform, then the Nazis would kill him."

"You think you're like a Sonderkommando?"

"I read a book about a Sonderkommando – at least I started it. In the book, the Sonderkommando comes back to haunt the dreams of a woman he'd never known. He came to her because he wanted *her* to seek judgement for his actions. For better or worse, Neisha, I *want* judgment. Not G-d's, not the FBI's, but yours."

That final word stands alone. Somehow it is not judgement, but *my* judgement that he seeks.

I can't wrap my head around his world of fate and blessings and prophecies. It frightens me. And somehow the implications are just too great for me. I know what I know. I know Aji is being framed for a murder he didn't commit. The criminal justice system is being bent in order to destroy him. Whether he deserves it or not, I will do what I can to defend him.

That is a justice I can understand.

I'm not going to be his angel of justice, I'm going to find us a place to hide. My mind scans through the same list of options I'd had while fleeing the bar. I rule out rooftops and empty apartments, just as I had before. I can't go to somebody's home, Aji wouldn't be willing to endanger them. Perhaps we can try to sleep in the park, although I'm sure a regular police patrol would find us.

Then I remember. There's a museum not far from "the Railroad Lounge" – the bar in Hunts Point. It's a little place, the Museum of Slave Art. I'd been there a few times. The last time, they'd shown me a weed-filled plot of fenced-in land where they were planning an extension. Maybe we could hide there.

I decide to keep walking, rather than taking the subway. The subway is riskier, and the museum isn't that far.

As we walk, the medium-rise office buildings are sporadically replaced, with housing projects, walk-up apartment blocks, a few empty lots and even single-story commercial buildings. We walk past an increasing number of little NYPD guard towers, hoping the cameras within won't recognize us.

I watch Aji the entire time, remembering what he'd told me: G-d seeks beauty in souls. Pain is just a tool in His hands.

I see pain in Aji. Pain I can hardly imagine. But I also see beauty.

As we cross the Harlem River, I realize that I know him better than anybody in the world. He might be the only person who knows me at all – even if the 'me' he knows is the one he seems to have defined.

I realize that all we have is each other.

That isn't what compels me though, as I reach my hand out to grip his. I reach for him out of loneliness or desperation. I reach out because I want his touch. As my fingers touch his, his hand wraps around my hand and he holds me tightly. Pain rushes through my burns, but I welome it. There's a desperation I realize I should have expected. But there's also a need I'm delighted to find.

It is almost six by the time we come to the front of the museum on a quiet side street at the upper edges of Hunts Point. The sun has already gone down by the time we walk up the short flight of stairs to the front door. The woman inside sees me. Thankfully, she doesn't seem to recognize either of us.

As I push open the door she says, "We're closing soon."

"I just want to quickly show my friend something," I say.

She looks doubtful. I reach into my pocket and hand her a $20 bill. It is one of the few bills still left from Alejandro's generosity.

"Okay," she says, with a can't-help-the-stupid shrug.

The two of us, unrecognized, walk right past her.

"What is this place?" Aji asks.

His eyes are roaming over the pottery, the paintings, the fine wooden furniture and even the rare examples of silversmithing. All of it is work done by slaves. Most of it was done for masters, although a good portion was intended for sale. Only a few pieces, like the pottery gods inspired by West African religion, were made by the slaves for the slaves themselves.

"It is a place to hide," I say.

I head straight for the back of the building. The museum isn't large, it doesn't take long. The rear door, though, is locked and alarmed. There's a little sign over it: The Future Home of the Slave Art Experience. I pull Aji aside and I pretend to look over one of the exhibits as I think about how to get through the door.

It is then that a woman walks up next to me, acting as if she too wants to admire the exhibit. She's a white middle-aged woman in an immaculate dress. She also the founder of the museum. She'd showed me around before.

Silently, she lays her electronic pass on the little shelf in front of us. She says one name, "David Drake," and then walks away. Drake fashioned the pottery we're admiring. I have no idea why she brought him up.

I pick up the pass, and head to the back door once again. I wave it over the little reader and the door clicks open.

Aji opens it and holds it for me. I slip through it and he follows close behind me.

The lot behind the museum is still empty. It is still fenced in. The only thing that has changed is that there are now little red flags marking where the rest of the building will soon be.

Aji closes the door and a moment later, we take a seat on the narrow steps leading down to the lot from museum. Our legs touch again, but unlike the night I arrested him, I allow the thrill to pass through me unchecked.

"What is this place?" Aji asks, a second time.

"It is a place to hide," I say, "But we're not the first to hide here."

Aji just waits for me to say more. We have nothing but time, so I begin to tell the story.

"The woman inside, the white woman, is a collector of folk art. She was a partner at a major investment bank. About 10 years ago, she bought a strange little porcelain doll. It was strange because it was of a grown man and because it was unbalanced. It couldn't stand up. It had belonged to a young slave girl who'd been killed trying to run away. Another slave had taken it off her body and kept it and over a hundred and fifty years later, one of that slave's descendants sold it online, family story and all. The woman inside bought it. Just another piece in her collection.

"A few years after that, she came across another doll. This one had been found by a servant's kid in a collapsed shanty in Hunts Point. This was from back when Hunts Point was home to mansions, not distribution centers and seedy bars. The kid had kept the doll. It was of a little black girl. It was also unbalanced. His descendants sold it too – family story and all. They didn't think much of it. The woman's husband bought it for her – he thought she might like it.

"Only after it was in her home did the woman notice how similar the two dolls were. She put them up against each other and they *fit* together. They supported each other, like some sort of 3D jigsaw. She dug into both stories and she worked out that the dolls were of a father and a daughter. Before his daughter had been taken from him, the father had made two little dolls. She kept *his* doll and he kept *hers*. If they ever met again, they'd know each other – no matter how many years had passed. They never did see each other again, though.

"The man escaped slavery through the Underground Railroad. He fled here and built himself a little shanty. This was the place where he'd hidden. His daughter, yearning for that same freedom, never made it. When all the pieces of the story were brought together, the woman in museum bought the site of the old runaway's shanty. She brought the dolls here. She brought them together after over a hundred and fifty years. And she resigned from the bank, dedicating the rest of her life to preserving the voices of those who had been powerless."

I glance at Aji. His eyes are tearing up. He breathes out the words, "They were reunited after a hundred and fifty years. And now, they inspire others. The Lord preserves lovingkindness for thousands of generations."

"Exodus 34," I say, my unique Sunday School education reflexively triggered. "Destruction lasts for a few generations, but kindness can be preserved forever."

We sit there for a long moment, thinking about that. Then I say, "Aji, you *had* to come here. There are those who will be cursed, yes. But your kindness, even your kindness in killing, will be sustained forever."

Aji glances over at me and I see something remarkable in his eyes. I see just a hint of salvation.

And possibly something more.

We fall asleep there, together, propped up against the backdoor of the Museum of Slave Art.

It is a place to hide, yes.

But it is so much more than that.

Help

Sunday – 5:54 AM

I wake up as the world around us brightens. Then I realize where I am and why and I freak out. In the space of three days, I've gone from an FBI agent wrapping up a case against a murderer to a fugitive hiding in an empty lot behind a museum. I have no plans, no ideas. No future. There is no way for me to turn back the clock.

I feel Aji take in a deep breath as he leans against me and just as soon as it arrived, my panic subsides. I don't *want* to turn back the clock. I don't want to go back to being the FBI agent trying to put this man away for the rest of his life. I don't want to look for his network – if it even exists. I just want to sit here and feel him breath.

So, I do.

I know it can't last forever, though. I can't stop myself from thinking, from imagining, from doing something like planning. And so, as we sit there, resting against each other, I begin to survey our surroundings.

In the early morning light, I can see more than I had the night before. I quickly realize our small touches of good fortune. The location is about as secluded as you get outdoors in New York. The fence at the edge of the lot is high. It has a gate, so construction vehicles can eventually enter. But the gate itself is solid – and can't easily be seen through. It is secured by a thick chain that wraps through two appropriately sized gaps in the material. The side of the row house on the right has a solid brick wall. The one on the left has just a few small windows – probably ventilation from bathrooms. Most of those windows are boarded up.

The place clearly isn't occupied.

It will probably take a good long while for our pursuers to find us here.

Of course, eventually they will still find us.

In a way, the little space is both a haven and a prison. We can't leave. We can't fight back. We can only wait until our executioners come.

I feel my panic coming back. I need to do *something*. I need some idea I can hold on to. Some small step I can take to push back. In my mind, I make a catalog of our resources.

Allies on the outside, willing to help Aji. I don't know how I'd use them though. A computer able to watch the world, but not the parts of it that threaten us. A public reputation that might help us – but only if we can stay in public. Once we disappear from public view, it wouldn't be hard to fabricate a story about suicide or attempted escapes.

And an informant. An unknown informant. But an informant who might be able to see what needs to be seen. An informant who might have resources we can actually use. *That* is something new.

As I sit there in the pre-dawn light, I begin to turn the question of the informant over in my mind. I need something to stop me from thinking about the inescapable.

What do I know? I know the informant said he or she 'didn't join the FBI to do this'. Of course, almost everybody in the bureau is ideologically motivated. The pay isn't great. That doesn't mean the clue is worthless. Many people have had a career of actions they have been proud of. This comment suggests, just barely, a more recent recruit.

The comment also suggests a recruit who had a choice. Of course, the FBI doesn't press men and women into service. As a law enforcement officer, though, the bureau is less of an option than it is an opportunity. It isn't normal for a police officer to turn down the chance to join the Bureau. It's an opportunity. The informant, though, seems to have joined for the ideology. For them, the FBI may have represented a step *backward* in how their career would normally be measured. Perhaps it suggests somebody who took a major pay cut to join the bureau.

The comment isn't the only clue though. The informant also got his or her hands on a copy of my college essay. I didn't submit that to the FBI, that person turned it up. It had to be in my personnel file. The informant has to have had access to that file. SAC Miller and the Director would have had that kind of access, but they are certainly not Aji's allies. People in the Human Resources Branch would, but they wouldn't be involved enough in my work to care. That leaves two options: people able to coerce or entice somebody in the Human Resources Branch to turn over the data – or people able to steal it.

I flip through the people on my team – those most likely to have felt pressed into a role they did not support.

There was Clara McGuinness, a long-term agent might have friends in the Human Resources department. She told me to interrogate Aji myself. Did she do it because she wanted Aji freed? Then again, she pushed hard for protection from the US Marshalls. Did she know who was actually going to be called? If she did, she was no friend of Aji's. If she didn't though? Then she was a genuine friend of mine – and thus no friend of Aji's. It is hard to imagine her both trusting Aji and demanding protection for me.

How about Bill Riley, the expert of complex conspiracies? He could also have contacts in Human Resources. Surely, in his work with the mafia and terrorist organizations, he's encountered single-minded pursuits against criminals with few things actually linking them to their crimes. A mafioso can be pursued for years before a successful prosecution can be mounted. I can't see him imagining Aji in any other light. He wouldn't be upset by the cadence of the investigation, he'd have been expecting it.

Jason Peters? He's friendly by default, but no pushover. He is certainly a networker. If he wanted my file, he could have had it – easily. If he was an idealist, though, he kept it under wraps. He also suggested that Der'nube concept of family was about 'violence, intimidation, group loyalty and following some charismatic religious crazy'. That theory wouldn't spring to the mind of a man sympathetic to our suspect.

That leaves Matthew Crass. I'm sure he's able to access any records and I know he took a major pay cut to join the bureau. He's a new recruit as well, from outside law enforcement. Any of the team might be a possibility, but Matthew seems to be the one most likely to have been the informant. Of course, the informant didn't have to be on my team at all. It could have been some clerical worker two cubicles over.

I explore the idea of Matthew in my head, holding it and trying to examine it from every angle. It seems to hold. It is not definite, but it is as strong a theory as any.

Of course, I don't know what to do with it.

At that moment, Aji stirs. He opens his eyes. I don't want him to freak out. I force a smile and, as normally as I can manage, I say "Good Morning." Almost immediately, I curse myself for how mundane it sounds.

"Good morning," he says. I realize in that moment that I've only ever spoken to him as the leader of a cult, a prisoner, a spiritual guide or a man on the edge. I'll have to get to know the Aji who says 'good morning' like any other person would. I won't know him for long though. Maybe this 'good morning' will be our only one.

He seems calmer than I had when I'd woken up, almost like he doesn't realize where he is. Perhaps that's because he's a man who wouldn't mind dying. At least that's how it seemed the night before.

When I look into his eyes, though, I realize that isn't it at all.

He's calmer because he's with me.

Rather than thinking about tomorrow, he's thinking about now. I find myself wishing for a coffee then. We could sit at the top of those little stairs and share a coffee. We could just talk, about whatever. We could forget our troubles, at least for a little while.

It'd be nice. There are only two problems. We don't have coffee, and I'm not that kind of girl.

I find myself speaking before I can filter my words, "I don't want to lose you, Aji."

He sits up then. He's still smiling, but I see a single tear falling from one of his eyes. Otherwise he seems so calm, so peaceful. His voice steady, he asks, "Do you have any ideas?"

I think I hear a prayer in his words.

"No," I admit, "I've been thinking about it and I don't have any ideas. The fact is, we embarrassed them, and they'll do anything to make us pay."

"Can we run?"

"Maybe, but they'll be looking for us. I doubt we'd make it very far."

"So, we just sit? And wait?"

I shrug, sadly. I feel tears coming to my own eyes.

He touches me with his hand again, resting it on my undamaged arm.

"I've lived a life of blessings and curses. Neisha, no matter how it might feel, I can tell you that *this* –" and he grips me just a bit tighter "– is a blessing."

I smile, on the edge of bawling.

"I figured out one thing," I say, through the tears.

"Yeah?" he asks.

"Yeah. I think I know who your informant is."

"Tell me about him, or her."

"Uh, okay. He's young. He's brilliant. He's a computer guy. He must have taken a huge pay cut to join the FBI."

My voice peters out, I really don't know much else about him.

"So, he's good at his job."

"Yeah," I smile, a bit sheepishly.

"Maybe I can help?"

"Go ahead," I say.

"He's deeply committed to doing the right thing, but mistrusts ideologues. He believes fundamentally in the importance of law but understands how it can be abused. He is brilliant but is humble about his own knowledge. He's a good man."

I think over his words.

"Yes," I say, "I think that fits Matthew Crass."

"What work did he do with you?"

"He investigated things online. He ran reports, associated various sorts of data. Tried to draw connections between you and the deaths we were investigating. That sort of thing."

"Maybe he became my informant precisely because of what he did. He couldn't find connections and eventually he was convinced they weren't there."

"Maybe," I concede.

"What would he do now?"

"Right now? I imagine he's looking for us. Maybe a bit half-heartedly, though. I don't know what else he could do. I mean, maybe he could go public. But with what? He has no evidence of our innocence. All he has is the weirdness that I went from being your greatest enemy to your closest friend. That's not much to work with."

"He already made his move. Back when he sent me the email."

"Yeah."

Aji just sits there. I can almost imagine him holding a cup of something hot.

"What are you thinking about?" I ask.

"I'm thinking about whether we should ask him for his help."

"It could be risky. And I don't know what we'd ask for." I say.

"No, that's not the question I have. Let's assume he can help. Let's assume he wants to. Can we let him risk himself for us?"

"If we're making assumptions, why not assume he knows better than most how to protect himself. Plus, aren't those who bless you blessed?"

Aji just tips his head towards me. He doesn't need to say it. But I knew how to protect myself and now I'm hiding in an empty lot and sleeping sitting up. Maybe I have been blessed, though?

"This is all very theoretical. What would I ask him assuming he was willing to help and we wanted him to do it?"

Aji asks, "What would we need in order to spend another morning together?"

The question is so basic, and so essential.

"Vindication," I say, "Proof that the bartender wasn't killed by me or that John Buckner wasn't killed by you."

"Could Matthew find that?"

166

"I doubt it. All the relevant records were probably scrubbed by people with a whole lot more access than he has. Like the cameras in the bar were. I doubt there's any evidence to find."

"What kind of people would do that kind of work?"

"Why?"

"Maybe we could ask *them* for help."

"Whoever they are, they decided to erase and conceal evidence. They knew what they were doing. I doubt they're the kinds of people who'd give us a helping hand."

"Maybe they'd surprise us."

"I just can't imagine it," I say.

"I don't have to imagine it," says Aji, "I've seen people seemingly wrapped up in such total darkness. And I've seen them redeemed."

Is he talking about himself? About me?

"Maybe we could try. But I have no idea how we'd find any of them."

"Would they be online?" Aji asks.

"I can't imagine them talking about what they do online. Not in any public forum."

"Of course not," says Aji, "But they might talk about what they *believe*."

He pauses, on the edge of another thought.

"What do they believe?" he asks.

"What do you mean?"

"I know why people in Garubia cursed me. They knew what I was. But here? Why do so many people hate me here?"

It's a good question. I think about it. And then I remember something from years before. "You have time for a story?" I ask.

"I hope so," he says, with a little grin.

"I remember being at a party once. I told this guy I was studying Art History and he started laughing at me. He was studying biology. He asked me, point blank, who knew more about a flower: some famous biologist or van Gogh. I knew what he wanted to hear, but I couldn't help myself. I said van Gogh. He got angry. Furious, actually.

He told me that irrational thought like *that* was exactly what was holding humankind back.

"I didn't really understand what he meant, not at first. I mean, I knew he valued science over art, but I didn't really understand why that value had to be so total. Then I figured it out. For him, there was just one axis for realizing what value was. The axis of science. Truth was the ability to show, repeatedly, 'if X then Y.' That path, alone, offered predictability. And it offered control. If you knew X led to Y, then you could flip it. You could say: 'If you want Y, then do X'. Van Gogh didn't offer that. Whatever van Gogh knew couldn't be measured, much less used.

"For the man at the party, humanity itself had to be put on the scientific axis. The equation was simple: 'if you want human happiness, then do X.' Any other way of looking at things *inevitably* had to conflict with the *scientific* way of looking at things.

"Aji, we like to think we're in control. Especially here. We like to think we can beat anything – through scientific focus. It is our superpower. As far as that biologist is concerned, you're offering ignorance and darkness. His fear isn't about you as a person – it is about you as an idea. You don't make sense. You *must* be a fraud. If you weren't a fraud, then the world you represent would be an even greater threat."

"What do you believe?" asks Aji, quietly.

I have to think about that. I could have told him what I thought the answer was a week ago. But now?

"I *liked* what the biologist was saying. Not at first. He pissed me off at first. But I liked it. It is intoxicating. I liked the simplicity and the power. I liked the sense of control. The idea that we could *solve* what had happened to LaMarcus. But van Gogh never quite stopped speaking to me. I *wanted* to believe the biologist, though. I thought I did believe, but..."

I trail off, uncertain when my beliefs had changed – or if they had changed at all.

"I think I'd like to believe him too," says Aji, "The power and the simplicity sound nice."

"Maybe you could say it. Claim you don't believe in blessing and curse. Maybe they'd leave us alone then. The true believers, at least."

Aji asks, wistfully, "But what would the world be without blessing and curse?"

I let that thought hang between us. Using my good arm, I take the computer out of the shopping bag and boot it up. I turn down the screen's brightness to try to preserve its already substantial battery life. Then, I try to connect to the museum's Wi-Fi. It's password protected.

"The password is David Drake," says Aji.

"What?" I ask.

"The name the woman in the museum said was David Drake. Why else would she tell us that?"

I try out combinations of small and capital letters and spaces between the names. In a minute, I'm connected. Then, I boot up the TOR browser Emma told me to use.

"How do we find them online?" asks Aji.

"We just start looking," I say.

I spend the next two hours searching endless forums of like-minded people, reviewing articles in magazines with academic explorations of the topics. Trying to find posters named Miller, James, Jim or even Diagoras that might lead us someplace useful.

Aside from learning that Diagoras Johnson doesn't seem to exist, we don't discover anything useful. There's no hint of a group acting within law enforcement – and beyond the law – to defend modernity. Whoever's involved is careful about what they do. I do learn the story of Diagoras, though. He was a famous ancient atheist. Once, when he was on a ship in heavy seas the crew thought the storm had been brought on them to punish them for bringing such an ungodly person on board. Diagoras asked them if the other ships trapped in the storm *also* had a Diagoras on board. Had all the crews on all the ships sinned in exactly the same way? The argument was a clever one, preserved for thousands of years.

History aside, though, we have gained nothing.

We sit back, resigned once again to our reality.

"What kind of man was Diagoras?" asks Aji.

"Diagoras Johnson?" I ask.

"Yeah."

"He *seemed* considerate. He seemed deliberate. He was caring, at least up until the point where he killed Mike. He was incredibly competent."

"He is an actor in a war. Was he a general, a soldier or a spy?"

"What do you mean?"

"Did he give orders? Did he take them? Or did he act on his own initiative?"

The answer is obvious. "He was a soldier."

"Did he plan to kill you when you went to the bar?"

I think back. "No, I don't think he did."

"Why not?"

"There were easier and safer ways to pull it off. He didn't need to have Mike involved. I think he killed Mike, and tried to kill me, because of what Mike told me. It had to be a decision made while I was in the bar."

"How did he know about it?"

"Maybe my phone was bugged. Or maybe the bar was. When he overheard the conversation, he came barging in to clean up."

"But he's a soldier."

"You mean he needed to be *ordered* to attack."

"Yes, exactly. How long was it before SAC Miller was on TV – with a cover story that seemed to be adapted to you getting away?"

"I don't know, maybe 15 minutes."

"Miller had to be told what happened."

"Yeah."

"Neisha, how are they doing that? How are they communicating with each other?"

"By phone, I guess."

"Yes, but on what phone?" Aji is smiling as he continues, "Could you make these sorts of calls on your FBI phone? Could you order murders?"

"Maybe," I say.

"It would seem stupid to me," says Aji, "When I was a soldier, we never transmitted orders by radio. We used runners. You never knew who was listening."

"Runners wouldn't be fast enough," I say. Then the solution hits me, "But burner phones would."

"Burner phones?" Aji asks.

"Pre-paid phones that don't have an official owner."

"Can we track those?"

"Not directly," I say, "They don't have owners. And you can't just see where phones are, not without special access."

"Does Matthew Crass have that sort of access?"

The answer is obvious. "Yes, yes he does. It's called the Ghost Report. It can associate burner phones and people. We can see who they called. We can figure out who's in the network and maybe we can find some sort of weak link?"

"Somebody who's willing to do what's right – but just needs a little help – isn't weak."

"You're right, you're right," I admit, "How do we get ahold of Matthew though? If I call his desk..." I trail off and ask, "are you suddenly okay using him?"

Aji grins. "To rescue us? Probably not. But to rescue somebody else, trapped in darkness like I was? Yes, I think I am. Who knows, maybe we'll be rescuing Matthew too. How do we reach him?"

"I, I don't know. We don't even have a phone, much less a phone number we can actually call. I mean I'm sure there's some phone software we could load on the computer, but this is the FBI we're talking about. It'll get flagged and he won't be able to do anything for us."

"He does have a burner email," says Aji, "He emailed me."

"Do you remember the address."

"No," says Aji.

"The only way to reach him is through the FBI. That seems crazy. We can't just email him. Same problem as the phone."

"Can you email the entire FBI a message only he'll understand?"

"How?" I ask.

"Well, only my informant knows what he emailed me. Maybe we can use that."

I smile at the ingenuity of it. Then, one-handed and with fingers that still hurt when I type, I open the anonymous TOR browser and set up an anonymous account on a free web service. I give it a name: theRailroadLounge@anonmail.com.

Then, I start my message:

> *I have the footage from the Railroad Lounge and I know what happened.*

That will be sure to get SAC Miller's attention. He doesn't want anybody to know what happened. It might also prevent *other* computer guys from getting involved. Witnesses have to be suppressed, not discovered. It is the rest of the message that speaks to Aji's informant. My words imitate, and obliquely refer to, the message Aji received.

> *I've spent a year helping Aji cover his tracks. He's made random patterns. This isn't why I joined his organization. I've found Aji's real biography. I could write an essay about it. He's a fanatic on some mission. I know where Aji and Neisha are. I want to tell you, but I need some kind of immunity before I do.*

"Does that sound like his message to you?" I ask.

"Yes, it does," says Aji, impressed.

I enter the email address for the FBI's tip line and then I hit Send.

Almost immediately, I recognize what a stupid thing it was to have done. Everything has to go perfectly. The message has to be flagged by the FBI. Matthew has to be called in to help trace it, he has to work out it's for him *and* he has to actually be the informant. Otherwise, we'll just sit here waiting until they find us. Or worse, somehow the message itself will lead them to us.

Oh, and Matthew has to decide he'll help Aji for the second time in three weeks.

I put the computer down but leave it on. I want to live in the moment, to enjoy my time with Aji, but the fear and uncertainty are too great to keep at bay. We don't talk. We just sit and wait, all the bad outcomes running through my head in ever more detail.

Then, a little over an hour later, two messages pop up on the little computer. I jump towards the computer. Aji watches me, his eyes expectant.

The first message is from an official FBI account:

> *WE CAN OFFER YOU IMMUNITY. WHERE CAN*
> *WE MEET?*

I ignore that one, replying would just give them more to follow. That and SAC Miller doesn't want to offer anybody with footage from the Railroad Lounge actual immunity.

The second message is from another anonymous mail service.

It reads, simply:

> *AJI?*

Irony

Sunday – 10:23 AM

Instead of reassuring me, Matthew's email – if it is Matthew's – just worries me more.

"Are we sure we want to do this?" I ask Aji.

"What else *can* we do?" he asks.

"We're hoping, somehow, to find somebody strong enough to help us. To get us evidence that we need to beat back Miller and the rest. It is not very likely to work. And whoever is on the other end of this message, it might not be Matthew. It might be some sort of trap."

"It must be the informant. How else would he know Aji sent the message?" says Aji.

The argument makes sense. It has to be Matthew, or whomever the informant actually is. I still don't know if we can trust him though. When he'd emailed Aji before, nobody had been indicted for anything – much less been broken out of jail. The stakes are a whole lot higher now.

"He wants to do what's right. Just tell him we need help."

I write,

> *Aji and I are here. He told me how he got my essay. We need your help.*

The reference to the essay will tell Matthew (but nobody else) he's emailing with me. A few seconds 'Matthew' responds:

> *I SAW NEISHA WAS WITH AJI ON THE NEWS. IF YOU'RE HELPING THEM, I CAN'T HELP YOU. NEISHA CROSSED A LINE WHEN SHE KILLED THAT BARTENDER.*

I feel myself wanting to argue. I want to claim, outright, based on our friendship, that I didn't kill the bartender. But Matthew and I don't have a friendship, do we? Matthew betrayed me to Aji. Friendship and trust won't work. Without asking Aji, I write.

Miller only told you about the message, right?

JUST ME. HOW'D YOU KNOW?

Because he doesn't want anybody seeing the footage from the Railroad Lounge. He knows what actually happened there. He just wants you to find whoever sent my message so he can shut them up.

There's a delay then. Matthew is thinking.

WHY?

You thought Neisha had a vendetta. Miller thought so too. Why else would he put a brand-new agent in charge of the task force? He wanted somebody with an axe to grind and he wanted it to look good.

WHAT DOES HE HAVE AGAINST AJI?

"What do I say? I don't know that Miller ever talked to Matthew like he talked to me."

Aji asks the question he seems to ask quite often, "What kind of man is Miller?"

I think back. Miller is perfectly packaged and perfectly confident. He exudes order and the proper way of things. It extended even to his desk – it was always clean, precisely laid out and under control. I type, in response,

Aji is chaos.

Matthew's response doesn't come right away. Finally, he says,

I'M SORRY, I NEED MORE.

I realize then that I have one more thing to offer.

Check whether Marshall Johnson is legit.

It takes only thirty seconds for Matthew to reply.

HE'S THERE, BUT HE LOOKS NOTHING LIKE NEISHA'S GUY... TELL ME WHAT YOU NEED.

I type out my almost impossible request:

I need access to the Ghost Report.

Three minutes pass before he replies. Maybe somebody has been looking over his shoulder at work. Then a message comes.

I'VE ATTACHED A VIRTUAL ACCESS PROGRAM THAT WILL CONNECT YOU TO THE SERVER.

I was hoping for something cleaner, although I can't imagine what.

"If I open this and it's a setup," I say to Aji, "He'll be able to figure out where we are."

Aji doesn't hesitate. "Open it," he says.

"How are you so confident?" I ask.

"Because my informant is an honorable man."

I lean forward and open the little icon. I don't tell Aji, but if I don't see the Ghost Report, then we'll leave the laptop here and try to find someplace else to hide.

A spinner opens and I feel like my heart has stopped. I don't know what to do. Is it real or fake? It is just a delaying tactic meant to freeze us until they can find us? Then, 30 seconds later, a login page appears. It looks legitimate. It wants an FBI ID and password, though. Matthew can't give me his. That's simply too much to ask.

Is it possible he has a spare?

It's asking for a login.

His answer comes almost immediately:

USE NEISHA'S

Are they just trying to prove who I am before they move in?

How can that possibly work?

WELCOME TO THE FEDERAL GOVERNMENT.
THEY LOCKED NEISHA OUT OF THE BUILDING
AND OUT OF HER LAPTOP. THE GHOST
REPORT WILL TAKE ANOTHER DAY OR TWO.

It seems like it could be true. I enter my ID and password. The system opens to another screen. This one is asking for a case number. I'd never actually used the Ghost Report. That was Matthew's job. I'd always thought the warrant-based access was based on logging. You'd see how people used it and if they abused it, it would come out afterwards and you'd get disciplinary action.

Apparently, I was wrong.

I need a warrant even to open the application.

"What's a case number?" asks Aji.

"To open the system, I need a case in which a judge has authorized access. I can't possibly get it." I say.

"Why would Matthew send it then?"

"Maybe as a delaying tactic while they located us."

"Or maybe he has a work around?"

We can only hope. I send another message:

How do I hack it so it will work
without a case number?

Matthew, or whoever it is, answers:

JUST WAIT

I look at Aji. He still doesn't seem worried. So, we wait. I barely notice my hand tightly gripping his arm. As the minutes pass, I get more and more nervous. I begin to wonder how long it would take a team from the FBI to get up here. 15 minutes with sirens blaring? 5 minutes by helicopter? Is all of this just a delaying tactic?

"Breathe," says Aji.

I look at him and see total calm.

"We've made our decision. We haven't been stupid or irresponsible. The rest isn't up to us."

"Is G-d going to take care of us?" I ask.

"I have no idea. I just know it is out of our hands and so there's no point in panicking." he says.

Aji delicately lays his hand on mine and I feel my fingers loosen. I want to ask for an update, to send 'Matthew' another message. But I don't want to lose Aji's touch.

Miller's men might be gathering outside the lot. They might already be in the museum. Our time might be up. But Aji's right. There's nothing I can do.

Reluctantly, I close my eyes and try to focus everything on Aji's touch. It's easier than I'd imagined it would be.

Finally, the computer beeps. It's a message:

7-39-NJ-43851

I move my hand from under Aji's and type it into the application. An instant later, the screen fills with data and options. Even given the delay, Matthew isn't good enough to have created this in the time he had. This doesn't feel like a trick.

I have to ask, though. I open the email again and ask Matthew,

What took so long?

Matthew applied for a warrant? What warrant could he apply for without attracting all sorts of unwanted attention?

Then I see it, simple black text in the upper left corner of the screen:

Case: 7-39-nj-43851
Purpose of Warrant: Aiding fugitive apprehension
Subject of Warrant: Neisha Jackson

I almost laugh at the irony. I'm going to use a warrant for my own apprehension against those people who most want me apprehended.

Ghost

Sunday – 10:57 AM

The very first thing I need to do is get my bearings. I know the Ghost Report is powerful, but I don't actually know what it can do. That reality is brought home almost as soon as I look over the newly opened program. It turns out it isn't even named the Ghost Report. Instead, it is called the Global Online System Tracker. 'GOST' for short.

I've got a lot to learn.

I skim over the various parts of the screen and bit by bit, I figure it out. There's a map with a little phone icon labeled "NJ FBI". Using a timeline slider at the top, I can track where it has been. I can also see who has called it and who it has been used to call. That's not terribly useful. But I do have one more tool at my disposal. Using the timelines slider, I can track the locations of everybody I've called for three days prior to, and after, our contacts. I look at Miller's record and see that he is in Brooklyn, not far from Der'nube's hotel. It feels a little unfair, knowing where they are when they don't know where I am. But I'll take it. It is certainly reassuring to know they're nowhere near Hunts Point.

Unfortunately, I can't go much further. When I try to see Miller's call logs, I'm informed that the warrant doesn't authorize that data.

I dig further through the app. I see numerous "Unknown" and "Known" phones that I can't track. They are beyond the warrant's limit. Finally, though I find something labelled: "Possible Subject Communication's Devices."

I click on that, hoping something will appear. To my surprise, I see three entries. Each is labelled *Possible*. Each has a "probability of association" score next to it, ranging from a high of 74% to a low of 47%. Each has a "time of last known proximity".

I look at the history of the top device, *Possible 1*. The time selector at the top of the screen shifts and the map shifts as well. Now I'm looking at the area around *the Railroad Lounge* at around the time

Johnson ambushed me. I begin to slide the time backwards. *NJ FBI* and *Possible 1* separate, but only by a short distance. *Possible 1* was waiting at the end of the street. Then they come together and move towards Queens along the Grand Central Parkway. I remember driving up with Johnson.

I point at the paired icons and say to Aji, "That's Johnson's phone."

I see the call log. Apparently, I can track the *Possible* phones as if they were my own. It has a short list of two numbers, each labelled *Unknown*. I look at *their* locations. One, a number he called dozens of times, didn't move at all. It stayed in a single location in Minnesota. The second was only on for a few minutes before Johnson called. It seemed to have been coordinated with him.

I scroll to the present and see that Johnson is in Brooklyn as well. There's no immediate threat there.

I look at *Possible 2*'s history. It flashes back to the time of the press conference in Foley Square. It could be any number of people, but I'm pretty sure it belongs to Miller. I scroll backwards, watching the phone move towards and away from my known device. I scroll back almost two weeks before I get a definite and unique hit. The phone was in *the Railroad Lounge* with me when I first interviewed Mike. It belongs to Miller.

I look at the call log. What appears next is a huge list of calls. Where Johnson seemed to have laser-focused communications, Miller seemed to reach out to a broad range of people. The number of them, *Unknown* after *Unknown*, surprises me. Are all these people part of the same conspiracy?

I pick one in DC and run through its history. I'm trying to line up a possible home address. I get a likely hit, a place in Chevy Chase, Maryland where the phone spent the night. I open another browser and try to find out who is at that address. The information is blocked. Home addresses tend to be blocked for people who work in law enforcement.

I realize I could ask Matthew more, but I don't need to get him even more involved. Anything *he* does on official FBI systems will be logged. Perhaps more critically, even law enforcement personnel are allowed to own burner phones. Definitively identifying them won't help bring them down unless I have some evidence of a crime. Or unless one of them somehow turns on the others as Aji seems to believe is possible.

I check in on Miller and Johnson's current position (they're still in Brooklyn) and then I begin to methodically work backward through Miller's call logs.

Aji asks, "Can I help?"

I think about the task in front of me: Guessing where various influential people may live and work, assembling a network of communications and correlating events I know about with phone activity. Aji can't help with any of it. But he can help with the most important task of all – trying to understand who might be willing to step out of the dark.

I go back to the phone that had been in Chevy Chase and we just start talking. We don't know who lives at the address, but we can see the house is a beautiful one. We can see the cars being driven. We can compare the sales price to that projected by real estate software – perhaps detecting the trading of favors. We can look for court records that reference the address, suggesting legal issues. And we can see six days of commuting to and from the FBI Headquarters in Langley. I try to guess who the recipient of Miller's calls might be. And I wonder why the phone's owner live in Maryland while they work in Virginia. Do they have a spouse who works someplace else? Do they have family in the area? Do they drive their kids to school?

We realize, quickly, that identity will often be hard to pin down. Nonetheless, as Aji points out, we can still learn about the target. We can determine whether they went to church this morning, to a bar on Friday night or to some other apartment or hotel on the way home. Do they change their commute, perhaps indicating paranoia or legitimate fear? Do they take the scenic route to enjoy the views? We can look for hints of guilt, infidelity or instability. We agree that if the subject is promising enough, we'll find some online phone software and call them. We do, after all, have their number.

We talk about each subject, trying through our very narrow lens to understand the life of a person we cannot identify. We try to understand what forces we might manipulate. Family? Children? Religion? Shame?

We talk each one through and then we go on to the next number.

As we pass through person after person, I find myself wondering what a life with Aji would be like. We're both in our mid-20s. If we escape this, could we get married? Could we have a house in Chevy Chase? Would I commute to the FBI while he leads a congregation in Maryland? Would our life have humor, or would he always be brooding in the other room, thinking about the heaviness of the world? Would he scream at night, reliving his life's horrors? Would he drink himself into an unending stupor? Would he be able to hold on to some part of his public reality? Would *I* be able to rescue him? I can't answer any of that.

We'll just have to make it there.

As we work, the scale of Miller's connections begins to overwhelm me. He seems to be in communication with prosecutors, forensics specialists, police officers, congressional staffers, intelligence agents, a prominent journalist, judges and at least one very wealthy businessman. A conspiracy like this must be built slowly. Each new member must be encountered and then slowly brought in and recruited. One wrong step and the whole thing could be exposed. For the group to be as strong and stable as it seems to be, it must have been built over years – or even decades. It wasn't built for Aji.

The thought is dispiriting. We aren't up against SAC Miller and a few of his friends. The network of burner phones is national and the owners seem like powerful and influential people. It is likely that all of them are true believers.

This is not fertile ground from which to draw informants.

I'd always thought of Miller as confident and directed. He had to be to be in charge of the New York Field Office. If anything, digging through his secret calls leaves me even more impressed.

His secret influence extends far beyond his public role.

As we move down the list, I realize that we have seen no chinks in the armor. Not only that, but we have found no evidence of any crime. Just a man with a remarkable network.

I find myself wishing I could have access to that number in Minnesota. The number Johnson called. The number that must be some kind of nexus, coordinating activities across the country. It is, however, out of reach. All I can see is those links directly connected to Special Agent in Charge James Miller.

As we work, our hunger and our thirst growing, I slowly submit to the reality that despite all the information we have, there is no way out of our predicament.

A few more hours in, we take a break and scroll back to look at the present location of Johnson and Miller. They're in Queens. They still pose no immediate risk. I flip to a news site, just to see what's up. We discover that, as we expected, there is a huge manhunt for us with officers deployed all over the city. The reporters share that law enforcement appears to be focusing on two areas: The Sunset neighborhood in Brooklyn (near the hotel where Der'nube is staying) and Harlem, where my apartment used to be.

It's what I would do, if I were looking for me. After all, you generally run to the places where you can find help.

A protest movement has also arisen. Throughout the country, "A Ribbon for Aji" is now a thing. Somehow people *know* Aji's goodness. Perhaps they have experienced his blessings. In New York, huge numbers of people have been seen in public wearing Central and West African robes and dresses. Every reporter seems obligated to share that the evidence against Aji and me is overwhelming and that the public should not impede our apprehension. I wonder if any of the reporters are a part of Miller's organization. I wonder if any of those who aren't realize that they are following a script that's been crafted for them.

I flip back to GOST, in order to check on Johnson and Miller's positions before getting back to work on the list.

They are still in Queens.

With police in Brooklyn and Harlem – and Johnson and Miller in Queens – we're safe.

For now.

As I watch Johnson and Miller's little icons move around a small area in Queens Aji asks, "What are they doing?"

"Who?" I ask.

"Johnson and Miller," he says.

"They're looking for us," I say.

"Yes, but where?"

I point at the screen. It's obvious, isn't it? Maybe African child soldiers are never taught how to read maps.

"No," he says, "I mean: why are they looking *there*?"

I suddenly feel stupid that I hadn't bothered to ask.

"Good question," I say. In my head, I rephrase it: why are they in Queens when nobody else is?

I scroll back through their history, seeing them explore a single location extensively and then jump to another. What process or information would lead them to these seemingly random places?

As the Ghost Report doesn't label locations, I pull up one of the addresses in a browser window.

Then, I freeze.

They are searching a museum.

"Oh, no," I say.

"What?" Aji asks.

I start flipping through the other locations. Now that I know what I'm looking for, I don't need the browser to know what I'm looking at.

I know these addresses.

The pattern is clear.

"I told Johnson that I loved museums," I say.

"And now," says Aji, completing the thought, "They are searching museums."

I nod dumbly. The police have rolled out a massive dragnet, but it is Johnson and Miller who are going to find us.

They're going to find us, and then they are going to kill us.

Beauty

Sunday 3:00 PM

"We have to move," I say, urgently.

"Where to?" asks Aji.

"Anywhere," I say, "We have some time, we can think about it."

Aji doesn't answer, not right away. Then he asks, "Do you remember the hotdog vendor?"

How could I forget the hot dog vendor? His food is the last food we've eaten. I ask, "You want to ask *him* for help? He's 60 blocks from here."

"No, no," says Aji. "When he fed us, he broke the law, didn't he?"

"Yes," I say.

"And if they found out, he could face criminal charges."

"Probably not for a hot dog, but in theory, yes."

"And there are thousands of people out there eager to help us?"

"Yes," I say, "That's why we have a chance if we leave the museum."

"But that's why we can't leave," he says, solemnly.

My mind comes back to Matthew. Aji hadn't wanted to use Matthew. He hadn't wanted to risk him – even though he was informed and capable.

Aji is continuing, "If any of them provides us with shelter, or if they lie to the authorities, then they could face prison. And if they see something they shouldn't, they might end up dead. Like Mike. We can't run."

"Maybe we'd be helping them, like we helped Matthew. You know, giving them a chance to escape."

"Neisha, the vast majority of people aren't trapped. Not like that. They don't need us to find their way forward."

Even before he says it, I know it is true. Aji cannot risk others to save himself. I both love and hate that reality.

"So, what do we do?" I ask.

"How much time do we have?" asks Aji.

186

"They're searching museums of particular interest to African Americans. They'll get here in a few hours, at most."

"And what happens if we turn ourselves in? To the regular police?"

"If we get lucky, they'll arrest us. They'll charge us with everything from murder to hacking Federal databases to fleeing prison. We'll spend our lives in jail. If we make it that far."

I add at the end, almost as an afterthought, "And we'll never see each other again."

"We're in a back lot, maybe they won't find us here." says Aji. His tone is more hope than realism. He knows how unlikely that is.

I think about the place. Perhaps our final place. My thoughts turn to the slave who ran here and lived the rest of his life waiting for his matching porcelain doll.

"It is a beautiful place," I say, quietly. Aji nods, not even looking at the weed-filled lot.

"It is a beautiful place," he says. I lay my hand on his arm, my burned fingers sparking with the love of it and say, gently, "I pray that it is a place of salvation."

We sit there, together, for hours. We ignore our hunger and our thirst and our growing weakness. We focus only on capturing the time we have together. I ask him about his mother, and he asks me about my brother. We talk about our pasts and even allow ourselves to share a few hopes about the future.

As we talk, we watch the little dots move on the computer. We watch them eliminating possibilities. We watch the almost inevitable make its way towards us.

Finally, we see them come to Hunts Point and arrive at the Museum of Slave Art. We hear their feet as they walk through the museum. Holding each other closely, we watch their dots as they explore the little place. Aji grips me and I grip him. I find myself whispering verses I learned as a child:

Yea, though I walk through the valley of the
shadow of death, I will fear no evil: for thou art
with me; thy rod and thy staff they comfort me.

Thou preparest a table before me in the
presence of mine enemies: thou anointest my
head with oil; my cup runneth over.

Surely goodness and mercy shall follow me
all the days of my life: and I will dwell in the
house of the LORD forever.

When they leave the museum, I look at Aji and he looks at me and we smile together. Both of us, together, are crying with relief.

Then there is a sound – the sound of a chain being rattled.

I turn towards the fence opposite us. I turn towards the gate. Then I see it swing open, just a crack.

In that instant, I know that our prayers have *not* been answered.

Prophecy

Sunday 6:00 PM

We don't have time to move. In what seems like an instant, four people rush through the gate. Johnson, Miller, Clara and the 'US Marshall' who'd only been around for one early morning.

I have no idea what his name actually is.

All are carrying guns. All are wearing gloves. Miller, who is clearly in command, orders me to close the computer. I do what he asks.

The man whose name I don't know rushes forward and seizes the computer. He steps back, out of the field of fire, flips the computer on its back and pulls out the battery. I'm guessing he's trying to make sure it isn't online and livestreaming whatever is about to occur.

That isn't a good omen. Not that I need omens to predict my short-term future.

Miller then orders Johnson to search us. Under the protective cover of Miller's guns, 'Marshall Johnson' frisks us for weapons and phones. His smile is lewd as he runs his hands up my legs. I barely notice as Miller steps back outside the gate. He comes back a few moments later with a briefcase in his hand. Thankfully, Johnson's search is brief. We don't have any phones or guns.

As Johnson backs away, Miller begins to speak. "You have caused a lot of trouble," he says I expected his voice to be self-assured. I expect him to be in command. But he's almost shaking with anger.

He continues, "Your little phone messages have convinced a lot of people. And your breakout embarrassed the FBI. We are going to deal with that. Now."

"If you kill us, people will still believe our story," I say.

"Not many," says Miller, "The way you are about to die will ensure that. What we're going to do is simple and straight-forward and you will participate in every part of it. You will cooperate. The reason is simple. If you do not... well, Neisha, I know you're not close to your mother, but I will kill her and I will kill your ridiculous pastor. It will turn out that your mother was stealing from the pharmacy where she works and that the Preacher has been selling her product to his church. Aji, your group of friends will die too. Sadly, a Mexican drug gang will realize that their nomadic lifestyle was cover for an upstart cocaine distribution network. The Mexican gang will ambush and shoot down every one of them. They will die in dishonor. They will be utterly destroyed. Do the two of you understand?"

"Yes," I say, my voice shaking.

"Yes," says Aji, "I will cooperate."

"Good," says Miller. "I am sorry what is about to happen has to happen. But we have to protect America from the past – from the times when people just closed their eyes and hoped for some mystical force to take care of everything – and for the supposed representatives of that force to decide what was right and wrong. We're never going back to that. Science determines what is right and wrong, what works and what doesn't – what leads to the most happiness for the most people. We have advanced so far with science. But people are weak. They often refuse to be happy. That is why charlatans can threaten everything we've built. Aji's campaign of mass fraud and intimidation, and whatever legacy he might leave, is going to end here. We will restore what is scientifically known to be right."

Miller takes a breath, barely containing his fury. Then he continues, speaking to me, "The process will be simple, as I said. This briefcase contains $250,000. It is the money, donor money, that Aji paid you to kill the bartender. You will pick it up. You will open it and you will close it. I need your fingerprints on it. With evidence of the payoff both Aji's reputation, and yours, will be left in tatters."

"Why not just put the fingerprints on it afterwards?" I ask.

"We can, of course. It is a bit harder, though. Your fingerprints have changed, because of the fire. So, we need new ones. And, as a forensic pathologist once told me... 'if you can avoid it, never move the body.' We want to make everything easy. We don't want conspiracies and rumors cropping up because of any inconsistencies that might exist. We want street cops and casual observers to be easily satisfied of the truth. So, you are going to handle the briefcase."

My mother in my mind, I nod dumbly.

Miller picks up the briefcase and walks calmly towards me.

I decide, in a last-ditch effort, to appeal to his morality.

"How could you, the SAC of the New York Field Office, be so willing to break the law?"

He stops short and snorts briefly. "*You're* asking me that. You who broke a man out of jail? Who impersonated the Director of the FBI? Who is a fugitive from justice?"

"I never murdered anyone," I spit back.

"If you'd done your job decently, nobody would have had to die."

"What does that mean?"

"All you had to do was tie Aji to a murder. A single murder. One out of 30. And none of this would have had to have happened."

He lays the briefcase in front of me. I pick it up by the handle. I unlock it. I open it. The case is stacked with cash. I close it, lock it and hand it back.

"Aji wasn't guilty. I couldn't find what wasn't there."

"I doubt it," says Miller. "You just couldn't draw the connections. So, I had to do it for you. I had to arrange *everything*."

"You *had* to murder?" I ask, challenging him.

Miller calmly walks behind me and places the briefcase against the building.

"I never murdered anyone before."

"Oh, you just gave the orders. That's not murder, is it?"

"You're asking about Mike, the bartender?" he asks.

"Yeah," I say.

"His name was Matthew Pienkowski. He had an agreement with us. He knew the terms. He violated them, of his own free will. Yes, it wasn't exactly a *legal* agreement. But as you clearly know, sometimes it is necessary to step beyond the law."

"And John Buckner?" I ask, raising my voice just a touch.

"Nobody murdered John Buckner," says Miller.

"What?" I ask.

"John Buckner was a brilliant man. A Mensa member, actually. He had it all figured out. But nobody listened to him. He had a blog that nobody read. He was a friend of mine and he asked me for advice. I suggested a sting. He'd write posts attacking Aji and when Aji came for him, we'd get the evidence we needed to put the Dark Ages back where they belonged. Diagoras shadowed Buckner for three months, waiting for Aji. But Aji never showed. Even Aji didn't care about Buckner's blog. Buckner, more than anything else, wanted to matter. The whole thing was his idea. *He* decided he would die for his beliefs and he would stop Aji Abakar cold. John Buckner was a *martyr*. But he left the completion of his plan up to me. And it is my duty, to my fellow warrior, to see his plan realized. I need to finish what he started. Now, let's get on with this."

"Why," asks Aji, "Didn't you just assassinate me. Why go to all this trouble? Why hurt all these other people."

Miller answers, "We used to assassinate people. Only those who were so compelling that they threatened America itself. It turns out, though, that killing a person isn't the same as killing an idea. We've learned that we have to destroy what you represent – whether or not you die in the process."

Miller pulls a gun from his jacket. "Now, Neisha, this is your gun. As you know, it is a Sig Sauer P320. It would normally be loaded with 17 9mm rounds. Sadly, you fired most of your shots at *the Railroad Lounge*. It has 3 bullets left. You are going to take this gun. You are going to shoot Johnson in the leg. You are going to shoot Aji in the gut – a fatal shot, but it has to look like an accident. After all, we won't let him be a martyr. We're going to make it look like *we* tried to save him after *you* accidently shot them. Then you are going to shoot the wall. The story is simple, you fired at us. *You* killed Aji by accident. And then you died when we fired back. If you miss any of these shots, your mother and the others will die. Understand."

I nod and taking the gun in my shaking hand.

Now, my new fingerprints are on it.

Miller walks away, his back to me. He's completely in control and completely calm. I think about shooting him then, in the back. I want to smash his conceit and his certainty. But I don't do it.

The costs would be too high.

I look at Aji. I need something from him. Perhaps what his own parents gave him before he killed for the first time. Amazingly, I get something. Something remarkable. His eyes seem to be reflect some faraway light. Then he smiles, finding some wellspring of joy, and he says, with complete conviction, "I know that this too is a blessing."

It is a prophecy, like the one Mumbato Yogula experienced. It is a blessing. I can't imagine how, but it must be a blessing.

I summon whatever calm I can from my training.

I raise the gun with my good arm and I fire the first round.

Miller doesn't even flinch as Johnson goes down, screaming in pain and grabbing at his leg. I hope I hit the femoral artery – I was aiming for it.

I fire the second round.

It hits Aji, sitting right next to me, in the gut. Aji barely whimpers, but I feel as if I am about to collapse.

Then, I fire the third round into the wall.

A moment later, I hear Miller pronounce our death sentence. "Return fire."

"Sorry," says Clara. She gives an apologetic shrug as she lifts her gun.

I stare at her, accepting my fate.

But before she can pull the trigger, a police cruiser bursts through the gate behind her.

Blessing

The wooden pews of the little church are packed with people. The yellowed walls are lit by warm lights in old sockets. The ceiling is low for such a big space and there are columns everywhere. The church itself is an amalgamation of basements from the houses above.

The whole place smells of old plaster.

It is a place of warmth and welcome and closeness.

Nervously, a young black man steps up onto the stage. He's maybe fourteen years old. He walks up behind the podium. He hunches behind it, almost like he's trying to disappear from the crowd before him.

"Hi," the young man says. Even with the microphone, his voice is barely more than a whisper.

"Bless you, bless you..." murmurs the crowd in response.

"I, uh, I uh, wanna tell a story before I say my prayer. That okay?"

He turns towards the pastor nervously. The pastor nods.

"It was, uh, five years ago. I was, um. Well, I run away from my momma. She was a user, y'know."

All around the room, heads nod in agreement.

"I was like nine when I run away. But I didn't want no social services or nothin'. I jus' wanted to take care of myself, y'know. I know boys like me can be used. We can deliver product and not get arrested. We can take money. We can spot. We can make everything work. We the child soldiers of these, uh, well, the crews 'round here. Well. I was nine years old and I decided to take care o'myself and I knew how. I got me a job at a house. It was a big house and it was all boarded up and stuff. It looked empty. But they sold stuff in it. Lots of stuff. And I had my job. I sat up in the upstairs window watchin' the street. I had an iPhone they got off some junky who fell fast. I even had a mic hooked up so I could pick up audio real good. And I'd FaceTime if I saw a cop or somebody who looked like a cop on the block. Y'all know how they walk, right. I was good at spottin' 'em."

The kid's confidence seems to be picking up with just a touch of pride in his skills.

194

"So, this, uh, crew. They paid me good. I had food. I had a place to sleep. Nobody bothered me. Then, one day, these two black folk stumble out the back of the building next door. It was early in my shift and I'd seen people come and go through that door – but never just sit out there, y'know. So, I turned my mic to 'em. I kept watchin' the street, I knew my job. But I turned my mic to 'em. And I listened to 'em. And I watched 'em fall asleep. They didn't see me. I was peaking between the boards over my window. But I knew they was in trouble. The next day, after I got up, I watched 'em all day. I saw 'em talking. They loved each other, clear as day. Don' see that often. And I saw they was scared. And then late in the afternoon those cops came. But I knew – I mean I seen it – I knew they weren't clean cops. They were righteous all right, but they weren't clean. I knew somethin' was goin' down. So, I started recording and I put it up on LiveBlast."

"I didn' know who those people were. But y'all sure did. The video spread, fast. Aji and Neisha. That was their names. Y'all know 'em. And y'all know who said what and when. Y'know 'cause of that tape. 'fore long some other cops, clean cops, showed up. They banged through the gate wit they cruiser. They saved Neisha. But they was too late for Aji. Y'all know, Aji died. Whatcha all don' know is that just before he died, he looked right at *me*. He was lookin' right at me when he said, 'I know that this too is a blessing.'"

"People was too busy chasin' their tails to go knockin' on the crack house. So, nobody messed wit' me. But that blessin' thing shook me up real good. I mean the man's dead. Shot by the woman that loved him. That's a blessing? I just thought, 'that brother's messed up.'"

"But y'know what... I began to think different. I mean, I looked him up. I remember him sayin' blessin' is an opportunity and the biggest one of all is be able to bless others." I saw these prayer sessions spread, where one of y'all gets up and says what they prayin' for and everybody else goes and blesses 'em. And, bit by bit, I realized Aji grew even *after* he got shot. Maybe he was right, for him at least."

"But I saw Neisha on TV. She was mad. She lost her job at the FBI and it all seemed to be fallin' apart for her. When things all quieted down though, she goes and opens the Museum of Lost. She dedicated it to her brother and to Aji. They all is dead, but she's blessin' 'em. So, she's blessed. It's messed up.

"Bit by bit, y'know, I thought maybe iPhones and money and being able to stand tall isn't all there is. Problem is, I ain't blessin' nobody. That's why I'm here."

The boy pauses. Suddenly uncertain.

Then he says, "I'm here to pray. My prayer is nothin' special. I just want a little of what those two had. They was part of something bigger, y'know. That's it."

The boy looks out over the crowd, uncertain how he'll be received.

Nobody seems to respond. There is just silence.

Then a voice in the back says, almost inaudibly, "Maybe I can help."

As every head turns, a black woman in her early 30s stands up.

The woman is Neisha Jackson.

Postscript

This book was sparked by a conversation I had with a woman in my community. Her son had lost faith. The reason was simple. He could not understand the horrors in the world. In particular, he could not understand the Holocaust. She wanted me to speak to him. I didn't get the opportunity to do so, so I decided to write a book instead.

It is my hope, that in time, my own children will learn from it.

If you've enjoyed this book, please share and review it.

I would consider it a blessing.

Joseph Cox

Personal Notes

- The 'Ghost Report' technology was most publicly applied in the case of the assassination of Rafik Hariri:
https://www.the961.com/cell-networks-hariri-killers/
- The New York Times ran an article about art helping police do their jobs better. That inspired Neisha's career path:
https://www.nytimes.com/2016/04/27/arts/design/art-helps-police-officers-learn-to-look.html
- The anger Aji expresses at G-d reflects my grandfather's anger at G-d. My grandfather would hold a Passover Seder and curse G-d. He saw the Exodus – the mass death followed by redemption – as mirroring the Holocaust.
- I have some personal connection to the idea of Neisha's life being remade by the death of a child. My own brother died in an accident at 7 years of age. I wasn't born yet, but his death shaped our family from then on. Others have told me that they believe he

died so that my parents would leave the backwoods of Idaho where they lived at the time.

- The story about the soldier's execution for cowardice can be found at the link. I originally heard it on *Hard Core History*: https://www.independent.co.uk/news/world/world-history/history-of-the-first-world-war-in-100-moments/history-first-world-war-100-moments-french-general-and-deserter-9256651.html

- The description of the Prophet's prophecy (and Aji's) comes from the death of Kalman Packouz, a family friend in November 2019. As was shared with me: "Friday night, at about 8:30, his wife Shoshana went to check on him. As she stood there, he opened his eyes and stared to a spot over her shoulder and uttered his first words in days (and his last words on this earth) - "Hi Ma!" (his mother had passed away a few months earlier). He then opened his eyes really wide and they began to shine with an intense light. Startled, his wife turned around, for she was sure that his eyes were reflecting some light behind her - but when she looked there was none. He then passed away."

- I actually removed the firing pin from a pistol so I could disarm someone without them knowing.

- The book about the Sonderkommando is *Returning* from Yael Shahar. I confess I didn't have the stomach to finish it.

- My mother used to ask who knew more about a flower. In a way it was the basis for her magnum opus: *Reflections on the Logic of the Good*. Many ideas in this book started with her. She used Monet as her example. I've never been a big Monet fan, so I used van Gogh.

- Growing up, our family doctor was a forensic pathologist. He always told us that if we killed somebody, we should never move the body.

www.ingramcontent.com/pod-product-compliance
Lightning Source LLC
Chambersburg PA
CBHW032001170626
46807CB00006B/2588